BOULDER VALLEY

A MONTANA STORY

EVERETT RIGGS

RUBY VALLEY PRESS

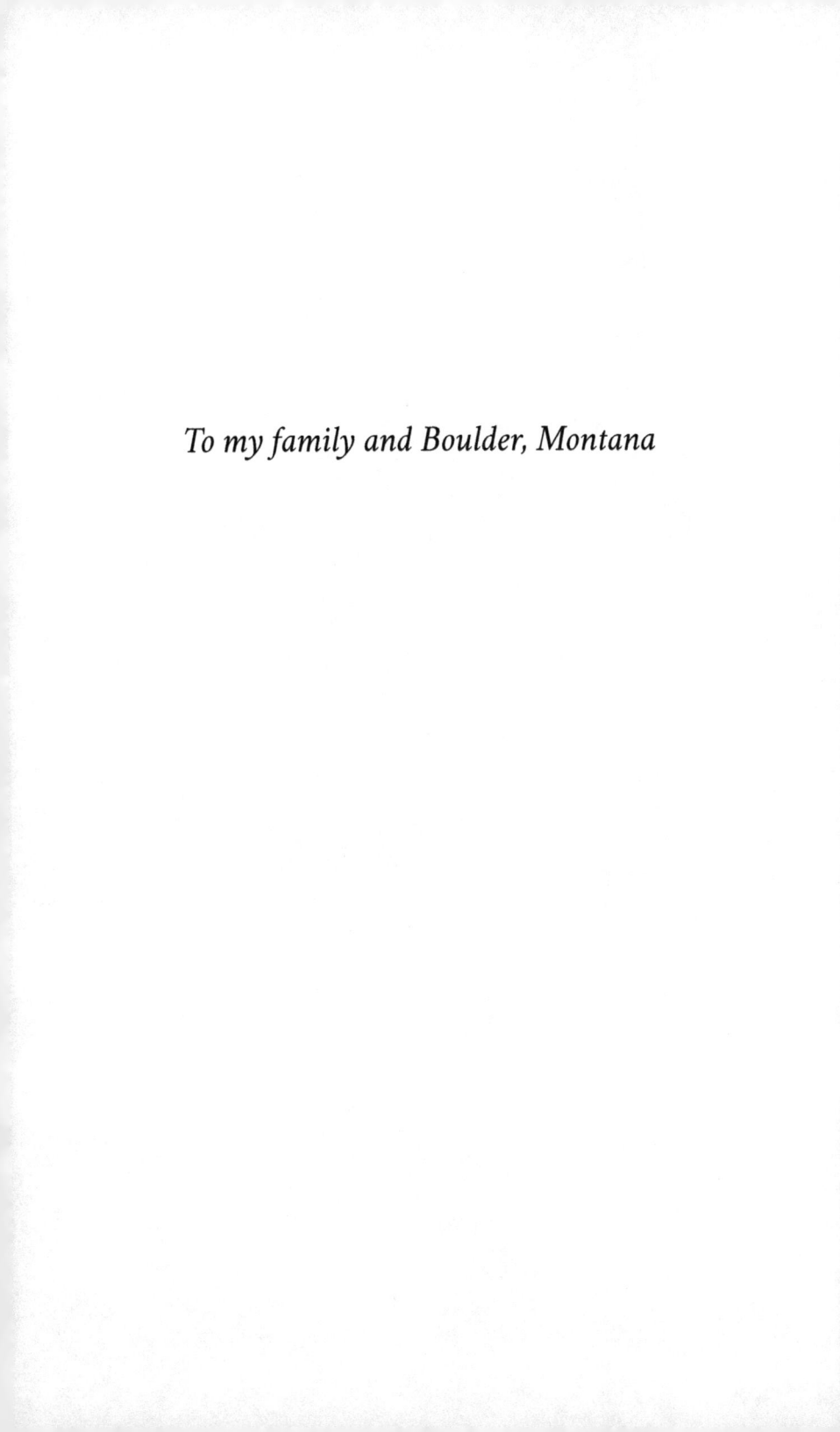

To my family and Boulder, Montana

SAMPSON STATION

On the north end of the Boulder River, in the Montana Territory, sat the town of Boulder Valley. It was a quiet town protected by its mountain environment from the rest of the world. It held tight to its traditions and way of life, resisting change with every breath. The Boulder River snaked its way down a long mountain valley, sometimes meandering, at other times rushing, until it joined the Jefferson River.

Those who lived in the valley were mainly cattle ranchers and miners; tough, independent people. Wild and free, but also willing to lend a hand in times of need. Boulder Valley was the trading center, the beating heart of the area.

The land was strewn with boulders from a glacier that had wormed and ground its way through the area eons ago. Many of the boulders were rounded smooth, worn by the slow passage of time. Others stood rough and jagged, defiant, daring time to change their nature.

Located at a high elevation, mild summers and harsh winters were the norm. The ground was sandy, not suitable for farming, but it held enough grass to run cattle—a wandering commodity that meant money and trouble in equal measure. There were stands of pine scattered throughout, thicker in the rounded foothills that stood in front of mountains that jutted abruptly up to the sky. The mountains were rocky and rough, laden with minerals coveted by adventurous souls who dared to toil there.

Cattle grazed on an uninterrupted landscape free from the constraints of barbed wire, and ranch boundaries were roughly acknowledged by various landmarks. Grit and wits were needed to endure, with grit winning by a nose. Firearms and an ample supply of ammunition provided a more comfortable margin for survival.

* * *

THE SAMPSON RANCH, or Sampson Station as the locals called it, was south of Boulder Valley in an open arena of mountains, rock, and pine trees. It was a working ranch that also served as a place of rest for travelers. The main house provided food, drink, and offered overnight accommodations when necessary.

The ranch compound was a relatively plain affair, cobbled together over the years as money or materials were acquired. The main house consisted of a large log building with two arms that had been added onto it. A large front porch ran across its entire length, with two rockers and a bench on either end. Shaped like a U with its arms oriented back toward the mountains, the building itself held sleeping rooms along one arm, a kitchen and dining area in the center and an office, and other common rooms in the other arm. The dining room and porch faced out toward the path that led to the ranch and was the primary entry point into the building for visitors.

Mrs. Sampson was the matriarch of the ranch. She was a fine cook and in addition to visitors, her cooking also attracted local cowboys looking for a good meal. Many would put in a day's work just to eat at her table. Thus, the laughter and lively conversation of people enjoying a good meal and companionship often filled the main house's dining room. However, on this day, there was only one occupant in the dining room. A rancher named Jim Webster.

Webster was a muscular man with a severe nature. He understood hard work well and humor hardly at all. His worn, wide-brimmed hat rested on a nail in the room's corner. An 1866 Winchester repeating rifle sat on the table, Webster's pride and joy. It had taken him a long time to save up the money to purchase it, and death was the only way he'd part from it. He also wore a cartridge belt around his waist with a revolver at his hip. The dining room's door opened onto the porch and, at Webster's insistence, was propped open. He had moved the table to look down the trail to the ranch.

Mrs. Sampson shuffled into the dining room and placed a steaming plate of potatoes, carrots, and beef in front of Webster. He ignored the proffered fork and knife, instead slowly drumming his fingers on the tabletop. She shifted her weight from foot to foot and nervously glanced at the open door. Her long, yellow-white hair was scraped back tightly into a bun, accentuating her thin face and downturned eyes. Her sunken cheeks, thin lips, and hunched shoulders gave her the appearance of someone who had seen more sadness than joy in her life.

She looked at Webster and said, "Is something bothering you, Jim? I heard you're leaving this area."

The rancher gave her a stern look. "Yep. I'm getting the hell out of here. Things aren't looking too good these days. There's a war coming to these parts, and I don't want a thing to do with it. I'm going to Ohio to get my wife and kids back. She's holed up with some relatives. I'm not from there, but I guess I'll have to make a go of it. Thought I'd have a good meal before I leave the territory."

"I heard you already sold your ranch."

Webster pounded his fist on the table,

causing Mrs. Sampson to flinch. "That's right. I sold it to Colberg over on the Two Dot. They deal fairly with people. Not like that buzzard, Branson Calloway. I doubt those Two Dot boys can hold Calloway off for long."

Mrs. Sampson furrowed her brow and involuntarily clenched her fists. "I heard Calloway hired the Stipic Kid to do his bidding."

Webster slowly nodded and said, "You heard right. The Kid can murder anyone he wants on Calloway's orders. Nobody can stop him. Calloway has the law in his pocket."

Mrs. Sampson continued, "I heard Calloway even controls the justice of the peace and the sheriff now."

Jim Webster lowered his head in dismay, his body slumping a bit, then he suddenly sat up straight and spoke loudly. "That's why he can steal from everybody. He ran off with most of my cattle on a fake writ, claiming I rustled them down in Texas. Hell! I've never even been to Texas and don't know anybody from there. People say those Texans are shady people. I don't hang around folks like that!"

Mrs. Sampson laughed nervously. Then she spoke softly and firmly, as though she were lecturing an ignorant child. "Well, Jim, I've met some fine people from Texas. They can get a little loud, so if a person is sensitive to noise, they might want to stand back a few feet when dealing with them. Other than that, they seem alright."

Webster made a dismissive gesture with his hand. "I'll take your word for it, ma'am. But I think I'll stay clear of Texans if I can. I'm not eager to stray too far off the trail I know best. Calloway came from Texas."

He took a bite of food and savored the taste. He was about to take another when he saw Mrs. Sampson freeze in the doorway. She was staring at something outside. Webster leaned over to look around her and made out a cloud of dust in the distance.

He became rigid in his chair, every muscle in his body ready for action. "Riders! It looks like trouble is here. I wanted to leave here without a fight. It doesn't look like that will happen."

"Relax some, Jim. We don't know who they are. Let's not court trouble."

They both stared at the growing dust cloud. Soon the shapes of several riders materialized from the haze, becoming clear as they approached. Upon reaching the ranch house, the men dismounted from their horses and the animals were placed in a corral at the rear of the building. They then dispersed and took up shooting positions behind various objects cluttering the front of the house.

Webster grimaced as the gravity of his situation became clear to him. "Damn, that's the Stipic Kid's bunch. He's the small one in the middle who ducked behind that log. It looks like they might do me in. They won't let me walk away from this. I guess I shouldn't have run my mouth about Calloway stealing my cattle. I'll see if I can take a few of them with me before crossing the river."

Mrs. Sampson wrung her hands and continued staring at the men outside. "Surely, they don't mean to shoot you in cold blood, Jim. That would be plain murder. They outnumber you ten to one."

Webster picked up his rifle and laid it across his lap. "The Kid didn't come here to talk, ma'am. You need to get out of here quick. They won't fire on you. Even the Kid isn't that low. I'll hold my fire until you're clear of any danger. Try to get word to the

Two Dot if you can leave the ranch. Tell them what happened here."

Mrs. Sampson cried out, "I can't just leave you here to be shot down, Jim! Try to make a run for it to the hills out back. Maybe you can get there."

He looked at her, worry in his eyes, and said, "I won't make it. There are too many of them. Please leave, Mrs. Sampson. My horse is outside. Take it and see if they'll let you go. Like I said, head for the Two Dot."

Mrs. Sampson wiped away tears trickling down her face. She straightened her dress and took on an air of resoluteness. She stepped onto the porch and the Stipic Kid stood up from behind the log.

The Kid pushed his hat back on his head. "Don't be afraid. Come forward. I won't harm you. We're here for that dirty cattle rustler, Webster, not you."

Mrs. Sampson pointed at the Kid. "Why would you want to hurt Jim? He's a hard-working rancher. He isn't a cattle rustler."

"I don't have time to argue with you, woman. I have a job to do. Come forward and get out of the way before you get hurt."

The Kid motioned for Mrs. Sampson to

walk toward him. She said a quick goodbye to Webster and approached the hitching post in front of the porch. She untied Webster's horse and started to lead it away from the house. Her path took her by the Kid, and when she passed him, he grabbed the reins from her. She'd never seen the Stipic Kid in person, let alone up close, and his appearance fascinated her.

At first glance, to someone who didn't know or hadn't heard of him, the Stipic Kid would invoke no fear. He was small, and although he was a man, he looked like a boy with his thin frame and soft, round face. This softness hid a wiry strength. His demeanor was mild and passive, but jovial and entertaining when needed. It was all camouflage that lured unsuspecting victims into a false sense of safety. All one had to do was look into the Kid's eyes to know his true nature. He had the eyes of a viper. Cold, bright, and intelligent.

The Kid wasn't a mad-dog killer. Few died by his hand out of anger or passion. Although when he was angry, he was ferocious in his wrath. The Kid did, however, fixate on certain people with an intense dislike that was the product of unconscious jealousy. Overall, though, he had the gift of blankness, and detached self-interest usually motivated his acts. The Kid could dispatch a person, then sit down to a meal without thinking about what he'd just done. That characteristic made him dangerous, and his victims often didn't see their death coming until it was too late. No one who knew him took him for granted. Mrs. Sampson felt the Kid's true nature, and it made her shudder.

Webster saw that the Kid had taken hold of the horse and wouldn't allow Mrs. Sampson to leave the ranch. He feared for her safety, and he quickly rose from his chair, rifle in hand, and moved to the doorway. He deliberately kept the barrel of his rifle pointing down. He meant to yell at the Kid to let her leave, and had no intention of shooting, as the risk of hitting Mrs. Sampson was too high.

The Kid, seeing Webster in the doorway with a rifle in his hands, struck like a rattlesnake. He drew his revolver and fired. The Kid wasn't concerned about Webster's intentions. Webster was there to be shot, so the Kid shot him. It was so quick Mrs. Sampson took a few steps back. Webster stumbled into the house, clutching his side.

"You shot him when you knew he wouldn't fire because I was standing by you." Mrs. Sampson's voice rose in pitch. "That was a terrible thing to do. You're a murderer!"

The Kid laughed. "I came here to shoot him, and I did. I don't recall any rules about shootin' folk. Now, come here out of the way until I finish my business."

The Kid led the horse to a spot on the side of the house out of the line of fire and tied it up. Mrs. Sampson followed and sat on a stump in a tree's shade. The Kid walked off, yelling orders at his men. Mrs. Sampson was too stunned to do anything, and the thought of grabbing the horse and making an escape didn't cross her mind.

Though mortally wounded, bleeding and struggling to breathe, Webster turned over a thick table and pushed it into the doorway. He took cover behind it and fired on the Kid's men. A fight broke out, the sudden burst of gunfire clapping like thunder around the once quiet ranch. This event marked the beginning of the cattle war in the Boulder Valley area.

ELIZABETH

*E*lizabeth Calloway sat on her horse at the crest of a hill overlooking the Sampson Ranch, quietly watching the unfolding drama below. She was interested in the outcome. However, it wasn't an interest born of any emotional investment. It was the interest of a business partner who wanted to make sure a routine matter was correctly concluded.

She dressed like a cowboy, but even at a distance, a casual observer wouldn't have taken her for a man. She wore denim trousers, chaps, a plain cotton shirt, and a Monte Carlo-style Panama straw hat. Her father got the hat for her from a hatmaker in

California who had learned to make hats from a failed Ecuadorian gold miner. A bright, gold-colored silk scarf tied around her neck completed the ensemble. Elizabeth was striking in appearance. Her bright green eyes sparkled in the light, and her delicate figure seemed to flow softly as if dancing. Her face, oval with high cheekbones, was framed by cascading waves of fiery, strawberry-blonde hair. She looked like a graceful ballerina, but there was a hardness to that gracefulness.

Elizabeth was always well mounted and rode a black horse that was a little over sixteen hands. Her saddle and tack were Mexican styled, as were her spurs, with large rowels and inlaid silver. Her pistol was a Peacemaker, and the rifle in her scabbard was an old Henry repeating rifle. Elizabeth was an excellent shot with either weapon, but her nature didn't predispose her to shoot people. She would only do so as a means of self-protection. She wasn't like the Kid. However, that didn't mean Elizabeth was timid. She wouldn't shy from a fight if one came her way.

* * *

BELOW, the fight continued. The heavy report of Webster's rifle echoed from the ranch house. Inside, Webster, who was near to collapse, gave the Kid's men more of a fight than they wanted. He kept a close eye for any glimpse of his nemesis, but the Kid took care to stay out of sight behind the log. He was a killer, not a fool. The Kid knew Webster was formidable in a fight, and he also knew he'd dealt Webster a fatal blow.

The Kid shouted to his men, "I hit him good. He's had it, boys. Don't let a dying man take any of you with him. Stay under cover and ride this thing out."

The Kid's words fell on deaf ears. The men had their fighting spirit up and took chances, hoping to get a shot at Webster. They ran from one spot of cover to another to gain a better vantage point. Ignoring the shots hitting wood surrounding him, Webster kept looking and praying for just one shot at the Kid. He wanted to even the score before he died, but he waited in vain. The Kid was too smart to let Webster have a cheap shot at him. He remained hidden and hurled insults at the dying man. One foolish man stood and exposed himself to get a better shot at Webster, and the Kid cursed the man's folly. He screamed at the man to get down and sit tight to no avail.

* * *

A GREAT DEAL of sweat formed on Webster's brow. A heavy feeling of sleepiness tugged at him, causing his rifle barrel to drop to the floor and his body to sag. But Webster was still in the game, and a spirit of grim determination revived him. His eyes cleared, and he raised the rifle over the table.

Against the rifle sights, Webster could make out the standing man. The man simultaneously aimed at Webster, but Webster's rifle spoke first. The adversary froze for a moment, then fell face-first, making a loud thud as he hit the ground. The Kid peeked over the top of the log and saw the man had met his end. He quickly ducked, and a string of curses came from behind the log. Inside the house, a pained grin crossed Webster's face.

On a hill at the back of the Sampson Ranch, Elizabeth heard the Kid's loud curses and commands. She'd just seen the demise of the man Webster shot. And unknown to the Kid, she saw that a new problem loomed—a cloud of dust rose from the valley moving toward the ranch. Elizabeth cupped her hands to her mouth and let out a high, shrill call.

The Kid's eyes widened at the call.

He yelled to his men, "That's Lizbeth calling. Something's up. There's danger, or she wouldn't have made that call. It's time to hit the trail, boys."

The Kid's men had also heard the call and knew what it meant. They dodged back toward the horses, halting their firing. The horses were carefully led out of the corral, and everybody mounted up. In the distance, the cloud of dust grew, becoming visible to everyone. An argument broke out among the men about whether to stay and fight or leave. The Kid put a quick end to the discussion.

"There's too many of them. Can't you tell by the size of that cloud? We've done enough fightin' for today. Webster is as good as dead, which is what we came here to do. Don't worry. There will be plenty of fightin' to come. That must be the Two Dot cowboys. You all listen up if you want to win the fight against them in the end. Does everybody understand?"

The men grudgingly acknowledged the Kid's words. The group left at a quick pace, with one man leading their dead companion's horse. They left his body where it had fallen.

* * *

JIM WEBSTER KNEW his time on earth was ending. It was close. A sickness filled his stomach. Weakness spread throughout his body, and his breath came in shallow gasps. His mind took him to a time as a kid when he went fishing with his father on a small river called the Musselshell.

They'd just walked out of a tall patch of grass onto a small strip of sandy ground next to a deep pool of water. His father put a grasshopper on the hook and tossed it into the water where the current ran into a calm spot. He handed Jim the improvised fishing pole and they waited. Soon, Jim felt hard, sharp tugs on the pole.

His father exclaimed, "That looks like a good one, Jim!"

Jim looked at his father with concern, not

wanting to do anything that might cause the fish to free itself from the hook. He blurted out, "What do I do?"

"Lower the pole and drag him up to the bank. See that spot right there? Drag him to that spot. We don't want to lose him." Jim's father pointed to the spot, his body tense with anticipation.

Jim impatiently replied, "Alright, I don't want to lose him either."

Jim stayed as calm as he could and slowly worked the fish toward the bank. Soon both father and son saw the glint of a large trout in the water. Jim's eyes grew wide.

Jim's father tapped him on the shoulder. "Son, you better hand me that pole. That's a dandy fish. I'll drag him to the bank's edge, and you get in the water. You reach down and throw him onto the bank when I get him to the edge. OK?"

Jim handed his father the pole. "Yeah. Holy cow! That fish is enormous."

He stepped into the water at the bank's edge. When his father got the fish to the edge, Jim reached into the water and flailed about, trying to get the fish onto the bank. He eventually succeeded, and both father and son celebrated, ecstatic at their conquest.

"By golly, Jim. That is one helluva fish! I'm proud of you. You did a great job. It took us both to get that job done. We make a fine team."

Jim Webster's head sagged forward, and his body collapsed into the table. The rifle dropped from his hands and clattered on the floor. He died with a soft smile on his face.

* * *

ONCE THE STIPIC KID and his men left, Mrs. Sampson gathered her composure and approached the house. Her approach was slow, as she feared what she might find. She called out to Webster, but there was no response. Nervous tension made her steps stiff and short as she carefully walked up to the table blocking the front door. Mrs. Sampson cautiously looked over the top and the truth was plain to see. Jim had gone to meet his maker.

Distressed by the sight of the dead man, she stepped back, turned around, and lowered her head. Clasping her hands together, a brief prayer was said for the fallen rancher.

She could do nothing now except wait for the fast-approaching riders. As the riders filled the area in front of the ranch house, Mrs. Sampson saw it was the cowboys from the Two Dot.

They pulled up and the first one off his horse was John Colberg, the young owner of the Two Dot Lazy C Cattle Company. In the valley, it was simply called the Two Dot. He was five foot eleven inches tall, strong, and muscular with a sun-kissed tan. His hair was a dark brown that curled and swept back into careless waves, topped off by a cowboy hat that was always slightly crooked. The contours of John's face showed a determination only seen in youth. His sharp angles and firm jawline highlighted his youthful power and strength, and his deep azure eyes added to the effect.

He had come into ownership of the Two Dot upon his father's premature death. John was a hard worker, an honest businessman, and liked by everyone. His cowboys were loyal to him and would follow him anywhere and through anything. He ran up the steps to Mrs. Sampson.

"What's going on here, Mrs. Sampson? We

were gathering some cattle in the area and heard a bunch of shooting in this direction. That isn't normal, so we figured somebody might be in trouble."

Mrs. Sampson grabbed John's hand tightly with both hands. "Jim Webster is dead. The Stipic Kid and his ruffians gunned him down in cold blood. You might've been able to intercept them, but someone called from the hills out back and they took off. I saw a rider join them as they headed out."

John placed his other hand over hers and squeezed gently. "There will be time enough to square this up with the Kid. He had to be acting on Calloway's orders. The rider you saw was probably his daughter. Do you know of any kin that Jim might have around here who can bury him? We can't take him back to his place. I bought it from him, but Calloway will probably have it by the morning. We can't hold it right now. Too much risk for too little gain."

Mrs. Sampson tilted her head and thought. "No. I don't know of anyone. His wife took their kids and went back to Ohio. She'd had enough of the frontier life, I guess. He worked the place alone, as far as I know.

His folks were from a place near the Musselshell River. I don't know if any relatives are still there."

John nodded in understanding. "I see. I've got a nice little spot on the Two Dot to bury him. Jim would like that. We'll take him and bury him there. I'm sorry for the trouble, Mrs. Sampson. Is there anything we can do for you?"

Mrs. Sampson stepped back and was silent for a moment. "No. I can take care of it. Just give Jim a good Christian burial. My husband and his men will be back soon. We can take care of the cleanup. I can't believe what things are coming to in these parts."

"I know, ma'am. This area used to be a nice, peaceful place. We'll return it to that soon. I'll see to rectifying the situation personally. Take care."

John Colberg helped a couple of his cowboys put Jim on the back of a horse borrowed from the ranch, and the group left for the Two Dot. In the opposite direction, a fast group of riders led by the Stipic Kid and Elizabeth Calloway swept up the valley toward the Flying C Ranch, the seat of power for Branson Calloway.

BRANSON CALLOWAY

*B*ranson Calloway changed everything when he arrived in Boulder Valley from Texas. Before his arrival, the valley was peaceful, and the ranches scattered throughout the area used a sizeable public range to raise cattle. An impromptu court of ranchers, a rope, and a suitable tree promptly dealt with any cattle rustling and major crimes. The sheriff and justice of the peace in Boulder Valley dealt with the minor crimes that occurred. However, Branson Calloway considered the Boulder Valley area an untapped resource to be gained, and he meant to take it.

Calloway came to Texas from England.

Coming from wealth and privilege, he knew no other way of life. Branson was the third son of an English baron, and being the third son, he knew inheritance of the family estate wouldn't be in his future. His father provided him a first-rate education at the finest schools. Still, Calloway wasn't interested in any of the vocations his father suggested, all of which meant to further the estate's position. Branson decided if he couldn't inherit the family estate, he'd create an empire in his image. He wasn't interested in playing second fiddle to his older brother when that brother became the baron.

A life of travel and adventure led him to the United States and then to Texas. Calloway became fascinated with the cowboy life. It was a life far removed from the boring life of endless parties, family politics, and the mindless etiquette of the English aristocracy. In Texas, Branson found an open country for the taking, with an endless supply of bandits and Comanche to fight, cattle to rustle, and land to grab. It was the perfect place for a man of ambition and greed to flourish.

And flourish he did. With his money, Calloway ran enormous herds of cattle in Texas.

He became one of the dominant players in the great cattle drives to the north. However, his name also became associated with stories of invading the rights of others. He never kept a trail boss who couldn't double the size of the herd assigned to him, be that theft from other cattlemen on the trail or raids into Mexico, which Branson liked to lead.

He was a tall, gaunt man with a stoic countenance. His speech was usually formal, but after living on the frontier for years, the style and slang of the cowboy crept in. Calloway's face was long and severe, with prominent eyebrows often drawn together in a frown. Long speckled gray hair fell to his shoulders. A large, hooked nose completed his face. He dressed as a man of means, but his clothing was always somber, usually black, the color of his heart. Clothing comprised a fine bowler hat, long-tailed coat, black silk tie, and black trousers. He sometimes tucked the trousers into his boots, depending on his mood and the task at hand.

Branson never carried a firearm. He considered it beneath a man of his station. He delegated tasks requiring a gun to subordinates, but that didn't mean Calloway was unfamiliar with firearms. He was a good shot and once killed a man in a duel over a point of honor he could no longer recall and, frankly, didn't care about once he completed the contest. It was the combat and conquest that excited him. Branson enjoyed hunting but had a gun bearer to see to his weapons. When personal safety was at risk, he always had a few handpicked bodyguards at his side.

Calloway wanted power. Period. A compulsion drove him to commit any act in its acquisition. Wealth was the means through which he could achieve power. Branson was wealthy in his own right but not rich enough, in his mind, to accomplish the empire occupying his thoughts. The easiest way for him to accumulate frontier wealth was by gaining new grazing lands and stocking them with stolen cattle.

However, if any person dared to accuse Calloway of stealing cattle, he was deeply offended and lashed out at the individual. Branson would loudly declare that he never unlawfully deprived a person of their property.

Through clever scheming and bribing, Calloway converted the local legal machinery into a tool to do his bidding. Calloway believed that if he controlled the law and had sufficient fighting men on the range, there was nothing anyone could do to stop him. He could cloak his actions with the appearance of lawfulness.

He'd been married a short time after arriving in Texas. But his wife, who gave birth to Elizabeth, died of a fever when the girl was still very young. He never remarried nor had another child, and his deep-seated disappointment at not having a son carried over into raising his daughter. He brought her up in the manner of a boy, taught the harsh ideals of her father. She was a means to help him implement his plans.

On her eighteenth birthday, Calloway declared to his daughter, "Elizabeth, I want you to be a fighter, always fight.

"Everything I have, I got from fighting for it. Fight dirty if you must. It's won me the cattle empire I now have and will get you the same thing. Be tough as nails and trample your enemy before they get you. That's life.

Survival of the fittest. There isn't much else to it."

Growing up in a wild country, among rough people, Elizabeth never really questioned her father's advice and training. She'd never been to a city, and the tribulations of the frontier hardened even the women she encountered in her life. There was no softness. Elizabeth's father taught her that the men and women who worked on the Calloway ranches were nothing more than puppets to be used to do their bidding. Elizabeth viewed them in that manner and felt their only purpose was to further Calloway wealth and power.

Elizabeth had broken wild horses in the corral, taken part in roundups, and was a top hand with a lariat. She could shoot accurately either on a horse or on the ground. Branson once let her enter a fight against a group of Mexicans who attacked a Calloway ranch, bent on revenge for the cattle stolen from them. Her toughness earned her the respect of all the men, including her father. In spite of the rough manner in which he raised her, she was only the person Branson truly loved, and her loss would've devastated him. However, he didn't see that as a reason to coddle her.

When Elizabeth rode the trail with her father to the Montana Territory and settled into life at the Flying C Ranch, nothing changed. She didn't question the actions taken against the ranchers in the area. These were everyday things to her, and it was part of the game her father played. You had to take from a neighbor by force or fraud before they took from you.

Elizabeth had been raised to follow her father's every word, taught to turn a blind eye to any wrong he might commit. But lately, a seed of doubt had taken root in the back of her mind. Elizabeth had started to believe that if her mother were alive, she would never approve of how her daughter was being raised or condone any of Branson's actions. Yet despite the doubts growing in her mind, Elizabeth's habits and decisions remained unchanged as her reservations about her father were not yet strong enough to break through the long-established patterns in her life.

* * *

Upon her return to the Flying C from the fight at Sampson Ranch, Elizabeth immediately went to see her father.

Calloway put his arm around Elizabeth's shoulders, squeezed slightly, and said, "It looks like we might have some fightin' to do in this country."

She looked up at her father. "We got the job done. Then, the Two Dot cowboys showed up."

"Remember, Elizabeth. In the end, we will prevail. We always do. We're going to take over this country and have more cattle than you've ever seen. I've already acquired quite a few from the locals. Sure, they're mad as hell, but I have the law on my side. I made sure I got that fixed before starting this little venture."

Elizabeth gave Branson a curious look. "How are you getting all these cattle?"

He smiled. "In a legal way, of course. Perfectly legal. When my boys find cattle with brands that look like they might have come from Texas, I get a writ of attachment from the justice of the peace, claiming someone rustled the cattle from my old stomping grounds. If I can't get the justice of the peace to write the writ, I do it myself and present it to the rancher. A little armed persuasion from the boys also helps; soon enough, the cattle are part of the Flying C herd."

Elizabeth frowned and looked at the ground. The little doubts had returned, and they rattled around in her mind, like pebbles in a bucket. What would her mother have thought about all this scheming? She tried hard to chase the question from her mind, but it wouldn't quite scatter.

She crinkled her nose and said, "What if the rancher has a bill of sale for them?"

Branson threw his head back in laughter. "A bill of sale isn't worth anything. At least not where rustled cattle are concerned."

Elizabeth gave her father a stern look. "But are they really rustled cattle?"

Branson replied matter-of-factly, "The proof lies with the rancher who has the cattle. If I claim he has a bunch of Texas brands I recognize, and I have the writ of attachment, as well as the boys to show a little steel persuasion, there isn't much to dispute on the rancher's part."

Her father's confession of, for all practical

purposes, stealing cattle from the locals didn't surprise Elizabeth.

She half-heartedly responded to the admission, "Well, it makes for an exciting life; an exciting life is what I like."

Branson's face lit up as he said, "More than that, daughter, it makes money. You will someday be the richest woman in this territory. It will take a little taming, but I'll get it done or go broke trying."

Elizabeth laughed, having pushed the doubts out of her mind. "You sure made a good start to the venture today, Dad. I rode lookout near the Sampson place and saw the Kid and his bunch surround the ranch house and sling lead into it. They got Mrs. Sampson out of danger before they started. Jim Webster was in the house and made a good fight, but the Kid got him. Webster did lay low one of our men, though."

Branson scowled. "They didn't need to shoot Webster. I just wanted him scared so he'd leave the area. I already had most of his cattle on a writ. He turned the rest over to the Two Dot when he sold them the ranch. I mean to take care of that Two Dot outfit.

When I get done with them, they won't have enough cattle left to make a good supper."

Branson was unhappy about Webster dying, but it further fueled his determination and he said loudly, "Killing Webster brings this entire thing into the open, and my enemies will be ready for a showdown. I'm ready for them, even if I must fight the entire valley. I can always send for more rough men from Texas if I need them, and I'm sure I can round up a few around here. There are plenty of those types around, looking to make a quick dollar."

Elizabeth wasn't as confident as her father. "The Kid was lucky today. He lost a man but might've lost more if I hadn't been up on a hill and seen the Two Dot cowboys coming. John Colberg was probably leading them."

Branson snapped, "I'll give that Colberg fellow plenty of trouble before all is said and done. He's the man leading the opposition against us. He's the man we must eliminate at all costs. Get rid of him, and the rest will crumble. Don't forget that, Elizabeth."

"I won't. Maybe we should've waited for Colberg at the Sampson place. The Kid might've been able to take care of him right there."

Branson calmed a bit. "We have time, Elizabeth. Plenty of time. The Stipic Kid has put fear in the people's hearts in this valley. By the time he sends a few more to meet their maker, Colberg will be fightin' alone."

"That sounds good, Dad," Elizabeth agreed, though there was a faint tremor of apprehension in her voice, "but we need to make sure the Kid doesn't turn on us."

Her eyes widened; this was the Kid they were talking about and although she didn't live in fear of him, the thought of fighting him caused her unease.

Branson was dismissive. "Don't worry about that. The Kid used to work for the Two Dot as a cowboy. Can you see the Kid as a plain old hand? They were gonna hang him because he shot the cook. The Kid said the cook wasn't worth a nickel and didn't deserve to live. He hit the trail before they could get a hold of him. The Kid has sworn to get revenge on the Two Dot. He'll be on our side as long as we pay him well."

Branson opened his arms wide, gesturing to the sprawling valley. "Someday, Elizabeth, this entire valley will be yours. As sure as night turns into day."

Father and daughter fell into a comfortable silence, contemplating the valley's beauty before them.

A SURPRISE

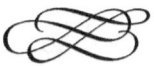

*J*im Webster's funeral was held at the Two Dot ranch. John Colberg had gone into Boulder Valley and hired the services of the only minister in the area. No one knew where the minister originated from, nor his actual qualifications, but folks couldn't be too picky on the frontier.

The amount of godliness the minister dispensed for a funeral depended on the amount of money one spent, and John Colberg made sure Jim Webster would receive his fair share. Ordinarily, John would've just buried Webster, but he knew Mrs. Sampson would be there, and she wanted Webster to have a proper funeral. The young rancher felt obliged to provide a fine service, and he knew people in the valley would be observing his actions. It was important to do things right, especially now. There'd be a church service in the ranch house, then the burial would take place on a hill overlooking the valley.

The site of the funeral service was a well-kept ranch, but not overly ostentatious in any way. The Two Dot ranch house was set in the colonial style, simple and rectangular, with symmetry being its defining feature. It was two stories, with a wood facade, a steeply pitched roofline and two large fireplaces on each end. It faced south to maximize the sunlight and heat that entered the home. A porch attached to the front led to the house's entrance. Another long porch jutted off the back of the house and wrapped around to a side entrance. The home was spacious and comfortable, immediately putting visitors at ease.

Inside the home, the primary features were a large sitting area on one end with a built-in library, and an ornate central staircase that led to the second floor, the only flamboyant display in the home. The sitting area had been cleared for the funeral service.

* * *

ON THE DAY of the funeral, people filled the sitting area of the ranch house, many of them heavily armed. The crowd was subdued mostly, and they said few words. Colberg and his ranch foreman, Odie Foust, seated people as they arrived. Everyone in attendance was a local rancher, and most had already suffered at the hands of Branson Calloway. The people in the room looked at Jim Webster's murder as a declaration of war, and from that day forward, the hostilities toward Calloway and his men would be open warfare.

Many other ranchers who suffered at Calloway's hands weren't in attendance. The knowledge that the Stipic Kid was working for Calloway cast a deep shadow of fear over the valley. People who would've ordinarily joined with Colberg to fight Calloway shuddered at the thought of taking on the Kid. The rumors of the Kid's deadly nature reached such a peak that the very mention of his name was enough to turn the blood of many into ice.

An air of grim determination hung over those seated for the service. Most had their weapons with them in their chairs, ready to use. A rumor had floated around the valley that the Kid would use the funeral as an opportunity to launch an attack. It made sense. Most of Calloway's main antagonists were in attendance, and Odie Foust was high on the Kid's list of people to take out.

John Colberg stood on the ranch house porch, greeting the visitors, when he noticed a woman riding her horse toward the house. There weren't many women in the valley and John knew most of them. The only one present at the funeral, thus far, was Mrs. Sampson. John expected no other women to attend because of the possibility of an armed confrontation with the Kid. He had been opposed to Mrs. Sampson attending, but she insisted, and her husband relented, so John bit his lip and let the matter go.

The woman's appearance confused John. As he stared at her, he realized there was something familiar about her. He racked his brain, trying to make a connection. Then it came over him in a flash. He knew her. It was Elizabeth Calloway.

John recoiled in surprise and exclaimed,

"What in the world is she doing here? There's going to be trouble for sure."

As Elizabeth rode toward him slowly, her horse moving gently and controlled under her firm hand, his initial surprise dissipated, and he stood still, mesmerized. Then, remembering his manners, John dashed off the porch to assist her in dismounting from the animal. Elizabeth sprung from her saddle so lightly that it seemed to him that she floated to the ground.

Instead of the usual cowboy attire John had seen her in frequently, Elizabeth wore a delicate black dress reaching the instep of her boots. A pair of silver inlaid spurs shone brilliantly in the sunlight. A black hat with a black plume and an upturned brim on one side completed the ensemble. The only color, other than the spurs, that relieved the somber nature of her clothing, was the white collar and cuffs of the jacket she wore over her dress. She had arrived riding a sidesaddle, which, like her clothing, once belonged to her mother. Elizabeth's hair, usually long or braided, was done up stylishly on top of her head.

A society woman with a critical eye

would've been able to point out the defects in her costume. Elizabeth's dress and hat were of an outdated style and the society woman would've noted that her hairdo was flawed and amateurish. Elizabeth, not possessing enough hairpins for the job at hand, had stopped en route and adjusted her hair on the fly without the aid of a mirror. But John Colberg wasn't a fashion critic, and the young woman's graceful posture and obvious beauty entranced him.

John took the reins from her and cordially said, "Go inside, Miss Calloway. The service is just about to begin. I'll tie your horse to the hitching post for you."

Elizabeth nodded, said nothing, and walked up the porch stairs and into the ranch house. Her appearance in the front room caused a stir among the crowd.

One man whispered to his companion, "That Calloway gal is surely here to spy on us. The Kid can't be far behind."

The crowd was angry; mumbling and grumbling could be heard throughout the room, yet no one spoke above a whisper. Eyes shifted in the young woman's direction and followed her every move, glaring with displeasure. The minister stood at the pulpit, surveying the crowd with a stern gaze that controlled them. Etiquette prevented anyone from speaking out or acting against the young woman. It was unthinkable and neither the minister nor John Colberg would have tolerated it.

At seeing Elizabeth, Odie Foust, a Georgia native, was sure that he hadn't seen such a vision since leaving his home. Foust was a medium-sized man, and although young, usually conducted his affairs in a slow, dignified manner. He had short brown hair and a mustache. His eyes were penetrating, reflecting intelligence and they were the defining feature of an otherwise plain thin face. Foust was usually genial in nature but could be fierce and single-minded when necessary. He was respected by everyone on the Two Dot.

Foust walked up to Elizabeth, bowed, and offered his arm. She calmly took it, held her head high, and Odie escorted her to an open seat. Elizabeth delicately sat and turned a serious face toward the minister. Then the funeral service began.

John heard little of what the minister said

during the service as thoughts ran through his mind. *They think she's here to report the names to her father. I don't believe that's correct. Her being here is the equivalent of declaring she's on our side. I know good and well that no one will touch her while she's on the Two Dot. What worries me is what might happen once she leaves. I better escort her back to the boundary of the Flying C. What's her purpose in being here?*

After the minister concluded the service, the men took Jim Webster's body to a high hill on the Two Dot overlooking the valley. Odie had directed the Two Dot cowboys to dig a grave the previous day. Once a few words were said on Jim's behalf, they laid him to rest. John looked over the valley and smiled. He was sure Jim Webster would've liked the spot.

Back at the ranch house, a meal was served. After the crowd finished eating, John told Elizabeth that he'd escort her to the Flying C. She didn't protest, and after helping Elizabeth into her sidesaddle, John swung astride his horse. They were soon off on the trail.

At first, they rode among the others

heading in the same direction. There was, after all, safety in numbers, and they couldn't discount that the Kid might appear with his men. They plodded along the trail until it came time to part ways. John and Elizabeth bid the others farewell and turned left toward the Flying C. The others headed to their homes and, along the way, agreed that Elizabeth Calloway was a woman of bravery. It was possible she intended to turn against her father.

* * *

ELIZABETH CALLOWAY TOLD NO ONE, least of all her father, that she'd attend Jim Webster's funeral at the Two Dot. Although on the surface, Branson and Elizabeth had a close relationship, she rarely took her father into her confidence. Branson was obsessed with schemes and machinations to add to his cattle empire, and he left Elizabeth to her own devices for the most part. Branson didn't monitor her comings and goings from the Flying C. On occasion, he would send a rider to shadow her on her excursions in the hills, but that was the extent of his supervision.

Branson believed his daughter to be happy. That was enough for him.

Elizabeth cherished her mother's belongings beyond anything else. She frequently wore her mother's clothes when no one else was around. Branson had kept all his wife's possessions, which he gave to Elizabeth on her fifteenth birthday. She allowed no one to touch them.

She possessed only one likeness of her mother. At Branson's insistence, one of his cowboys in Texas had executed a drawing. The cowboy possessed an exceptional talent for drawing, and the likeness he produced was superb. Elizabeth liked to take the sketch and reproduce her mother's look from head to toe. She pretended she was a society woman, waiting to attend a ball or another important function. She wanted to be anything other than her usual uncontrolled, wild self. Elizabeth's favorite activity was riding about the Flying C on her mother's sidesaddle when her father was gone. It was her father's favorite memento, one that he had purchased for Elizabeth's mother shortly after they had been married, made by the finest saddle maker in Texas.

Elizabeth's attendance at Jim Webster's funeral was an impulse. An impulse driven by the tiny doubts that had begun to take hold in her mind, although she wouldn't have admitted to it. In addition, Webster fascinated her because he displayed grit in furtherance of a doomed cause. Few men dared to stand up to her father. In Elizabeth's world, showing gameness in the face of adversity meant almost everything, and Jim Webster had demonstrated it in full. She felt compelled to pay homage to such a brave man, even if he counted among her father's enemies.

JOHN COLBERG KNEW none of those things as he rode along at Elizabeth's side. He only knew people would view Elizabeth as beautiful in any setting, and he couldn't take his eyes off her. She gracefully swayed with her horse's every movement, moving in time with it. Despite living an outdoor life, he noted her face seemed untouched by the elements. It was smooth and lightly tanned, free from lines or blemishes. He caught Elizabeth taking a quick glance at him and saw she was smiling. John realized Elizabeth knew he was staring at her. He glanced into the distance, embarrassed. Then, looked back at her.

"Attending Webster's funeral today was a foolish thing to do. It could've gone bad. What were you thinking?"

Elizabeth laughed and replied, "Well, I was sure you'd come to my aid if anything bad happened. After all, it's your ranch."

John continued with his lecture, "Yes, it is my ranch, and no one will do a thing to you while you're on it. The problem was what might have happened once you left. Most people at that funeral think your father sent you to spy on them."

Elizabeth didn't appreciate being lectured, and anger crept into her voice. "Let them think what they want! What do I care? I came to the funeral because I respect men with grit, and Jim Webster had a lot. I don't care that he was fighting against the Flying C. I disagree with the Kid shooting him. It wasn't necessary."

"I believe you, but most people at that funeral probably wouldn't. You took a big risk."

She shrugged, dismissive of any risk taken

in attending the funeral. "I've been taking big risks all my life. That's nothing new to me. I've fought Mexican bandits and seen Comanche. A bunch of frontier cattle grazers don't scare me. Why do you believe me when you don't think the others would?"

Elizabeth's frank manner flustered John, and he wasn't sure how to handle it.

He blurted out, "You don't look like a liar to me. I guess that's it. You sure don't act like a normal woman, though."

Elizabeth's eyes widened at John's statement. "A normal woman? I doubt you've ever seen a normal woman living with these people on the frontier. How do you know I'm not a normal woman? What do you mean?"

John blushed and was silent. He realized he had made a mistake.

She waited for a few moments for a reply to her questions, and when none came said, "Oh, I understand. You people all gossip about me wearing cowboy clothes, riding in a cowboy saddle, and shooting guns, don't you? I guess those pursuits are just for men, and normal women don't do those things around here. I didn't take you for a man who the gossip of fools would influence."

John spoke softly, not wanting to further antagonize the young woman. "I haven't heard any gossip about you."

Elizabeth didn't believe him. "Sure, you haven't. I guess I stand guilty as charged. I'm not a normal woman. At least for these parts. But I don't like people thinking I'm spying on them. I'm not a spy. If these people are foolish enough to take on my father, they'll hurt plenty, but I won't be telling him anything about anybody."

John pleaded with her, "If you have any influence over your father, you need to get him to stop his antics in this valley. A lot of good people have been hurt, and more likely will. There's no need for it. This situation must end before it gets out of control."

She sat up in the saddle, her entire body defiant, her eyes bright and threatening to burn a hole right through him. "A Calloway never quits and slinks away! Come and try to capture my father if you think you can do it. You all know he never carries a gun. If there is to be a war in this valley, the Flying C will win."

John Colberg was done being polite. The behavior of Elizabeth astounded him. He had never encountered her type, and the conversation degraded into an argument.

He snapped at her, "The war is well underway. The folks in the valley will never forget Jim Webster's murder. You can count on that."

"Then things are even now. Webster killed one of the Flying C boys!"

John yelled at her, "You don't get it! Your father took Webster's cattle, just as he has done to others in the valley, using fake writs of attachment. He claims they rustled the cattle from Texas, which is ridiculous! Jim Webster never rustled a cow in his life. But your father, all for power and greed, stole his livelihood and tried to run him out of the valley. Then, he had the Kid kill him before the man could even leave."

Elizabeth was unaffected by the yelling and her voice took on a petulant tone. "Who's to say they weren't rustled cattle? My father knows Texas brands like the back of his hand. Someone might have rustled the cattle before they sold them to Webster."

John shook his head in dismay. "I can see there's no point arguing with you. The plain, simple truth is that unless your father quits his actions in this valley, many people will die."

Elizabeth remained defiant. "If push comes to shove, I guarantee my father will be ready. With the Stipic Kid on our side, I'd say you're the one in trouble."

John pointed a finger at Elizabeth. "Hiring the Kid was a fool thing to do! That character is nothing more than a cold-blooded killer. He doesn't have any loyalty to anyone and keeping him around may come back to bite your father. He's got a price on his head, and if the sheriff in this valley weren't in your father's pocket, the Kid would be hanging from a tree right now."

Elizabeth's mood changed quickly. Her tone had been petulant and defiant, but now it became light and flirty. "Well, Mr. Colberg. You sure are a man of violent ways. I'll have to make sure I don't run afoul of you someday. I'm not sure what you would do to me."

John was stunned by her sudden change of mood. She had appeared angry only a moment before, then had flipped without any apparent reason. Thoughts raced through his mind.

She sure is a strange one. I've never met the

likes of her. Is this an act she's putting on to confuse me? She's a fighter, though, and she's beautiful. I don't think I've seen a more beautiful woman. I really like her. I can't help it, even though I feel like I shouldn't. Damn her.

Elizabeth stopped her horse. "It's time for you to take your leave, Mr. Colberg. We've reached the Flying C boundary, and I'm across the danger line. I'd hate for anything to happen to you after escorting me back to the ranch. I'm not low enough to lead you into a trap on our side, even though you're quite an argumentative fellow. It must've been something you learned as a child. I suspect you cannot prevent yourself from arguing, even though most young men escorting a lady wouldn't engage in such debates."

John laughed and shook his head. "It was my pleasure to escort you, Miss Calloway. I don't believe you're a spy. I take you as a straight shooter. Maybe we can be friends?"

Elizabeth moved her horse close to him, reaching out to shake his hand. "All right, Mr. Colberg. Friends it is."

John took her hand and shook it, then a thought entered his mind, and he spoke quickly. "If you meet me here in a week's time, I promise not to lecture or argue with you. We'll just talk about pleasant things. I'll hang out in that bunch of trees over there and wave my handkerchief when I see you coming."

Elizabeth smiled and said, "Maybe you will see me, maybe you won't. It all depends on how you behave in the meantime. You might want to take some lessons on how to interact with a lady."

With that, Elizabeth spurred her horse and took off down the trail. Reaching the top of a gentle hill, she stopped on the crest, and faced John. She waved her hand a few moments before riding out of sight.

TURNABOUT

*J*ohn and Elizabeth met several times. The more John got to know her, the more enthralled with her he became. John couldn't reconcile the contradictions in her personality, however, and it bothered him. Her father's activities didn't seem to faze Elizabeth at all, including killing men if necessary. John realized Elizabeth was fiercely loyal to her father, and he steered clear of any talk that might challenge that loyalty. He also knew Branson had successfully lined up the local legal apparatus on the Flying C's side. John knew things would get tough for everyone opposed to Branson Calloway, and he thought the meetings might be a waste of time, as any relationship with Elizabeth was doomed to failure. He was also concerned about what people might think and do if they discovered he'd been seeing her secretly. Despite those misgivings, John knew he couldn't stay away from Elizabeth. He had to be around her, to hell with the consequences.

* * *

BUCK JOHNSON WAS the sheriff in Boulder Valley and was a pliable man. The justice of the peace was openly corrupt. His court issued whatever legal proclamations Branson Calloway required to achieve his aims. Sheriff Johnson served the legal documents produced by the judge and left the enforcement to Branson's men. John Colberg approached Johnson, letting him know he intended to appeal to higher territorial authorities regarding the valley's situation, and that he'd see to him being removed from office unless the sheriff paid more regard to the law.

This didn't have the effect John intended; Sheriff Johnson didn't change his ways. Instead, he immediately ran to Branson and informed him of Colberg's intentions.

When he arrived at the Flying C, Johnson breathlessly told Branson, "Mr. Calloway, you're gettin' too heavy-handed in the valley. Colberg is fixin' to appeal to higher authorities. It's hard to tell how the wind is blowin' and a lawman must appear to be on the right side of things."

Branson rolled his eyes, disgusted with Johnson. Branson knew the sheriff would sell him out in a heartbeat and couldn't care less about right or wrong. Branson spoke firmly. "Johnson, I pay you to have the wind blow in my favor. I don't need men afraid of a little opposition who can't decide which side they're on. I can't have that. But you're probably right. I'll cool things down a bit and see what happens."

Calloway backed off and let things settle down. This surprised Sheriff Johnson, who had never known Branson Calloway to give an inch on any matter. Johnson assumed Branson had another scheme in mind, and the sheriff's only worry was whether he would be able to benefit from it. The valley became calm again, but there was tension in the air. Nobody thought the peace would last long.

During the lull, John and Elizabeth continued meeting. The situation threatened to turn into a full-blown romance. John didn't dare tell Elizabeth how he was feeling about her, nor did she express her feelings about him. But it would've been obvious to anyone observing them that the pair were more than just friends. They chatted casually about neighborhood affairs and other things, never broaching the subject of the looming range war. Each knew the relative calm that settled over the valley could end at any moment, potentially bringing them into opposition.

John would bring Elizabeth books to read from the library on the Two Dot. John's father had been an avid reader and passed the trait to his son. Although Elizabeth had lived her entire life in wild places, her father ensured she received a basic education. Reading was a common interest the two shared, and they enjoyed discussing the books Elizabeth read. Although Elizabeth could read well and enjoyed the activity, books hadn't figured in Branson Calloway's schemes. The books she possessed had belonged to her mother. They were few, and the sudden treasure of reading material delighted her.

* * *

RIDING to a meeting with Elizabeth a month after the lull in the valley, John Colberg turned his horse from the trail into the stand of trees that served as their meeting spot. He'd been riding hard. Dust covered him from head to toe, and John's horse sweated heavily from exertion. He reined the animal to a stop, not even bothering to wave as he approached. Elizabeth had been reading a book when John arrived. She glanced up, rose, and walked up to the heavily breathing animal, patting it gently on the neck. She slipped the text into a saddlebag and took John's hand after he dismounted, attempting to comfort him. Something was clearly off.

Elizabeth frowned slightly and said, "It looks like you've had a hard ride. That horse looks frightful. You must've been in a big hurry to see me."

John's manner didn't change, and he said tersely, "It was a hard ride."

Elizabeth changed the subject, thinking it

might improve his mood. "I liked the book about King Arthur. Chivalry and such matters. Although it might be better just to get the job done. Honor could be a hindrance."

John didn't respond. He certainly didn't want to talk about books, so Elizabeth cut to the chase. "Hey, what's the matter?"

"It's bad. Real bad. The Kid and his men murdered two ranchers a little out of Boulder Valley this morning."

Elizabeth was surprised. "How do you know? What's the evidence?"

"There were witnesses. A couple of boys playing off the trail saw it happen. Thankfully, the Kid didn't see them. They said they saw the ranchers stop a wagon on the trail. The boys were about to exit the woods to greet them when the Kid rode up with his men. The boys ducked behind a log, then peeked over the top. They said the Kid asked the ranchers if they were for or against the Flying C. When the ranchers didn't answer, the Kid shot them."

Elizabeth threw her hands up and said, "My father can't be held responsible for the Kid's actions. Is that where you're going with this?"

John responded quickly and his voice rose. "The problem is the Stipic Kid and his henchmen work for the Flying C, so your father bears some responsibility. Arrest warrants will be served, and your father's name is on one of them."

"What?" Elizabeth recoiled at this news, then the truth dawned on her. She replied angrily, "Wait a minute! How do you know they've issued warrants?"

John hesitated. Elizabeth had never been more desirable to him. She wore cowboy clothes without a hat, and her hair danced in the warm wind. Her anger made her eyes luminous, and they pierced right through him. She seemed perfect. A thought entered his mind. Maybe she appeared so desirable because he was about to lose her.

He spoke to Elizabeth gently, knowing he was treading on uncertain ground. "Please listen to what I'm about to say. Hear me out to the end. OK?"

Elizabeth crossed her arms. "Alright. What is it?"

"I think I might be fallin' for you hard. What I mean to say is that I might be in love with you. The time I've spent with you is better than any other time in my life. I've been thinking about it a lot, and I wanted you to know this, even if you turn your back on me for good."

Before Elizabeth could respond to his declaration of love, John took her in his arms and kissed her. He could feel her relax for a moment, then she pulled away and let out an exasperated laugh.

"Good Lord! You are a beastly fellow, John Colberg! Taking what you want from a defenseless woman."

John laughed at the absurdity of Elizabeth being defenseless. "Whatever you are, you certainly aren't defenseless. I'm serious now. Do you love me too?"

Elizabeth looked at the ground and kicked it with her boot. "Why do I need to answer that question? You know the truth, sure enough. I've met nobody quite like you. If you weren't so impolite, I might even say you were like the knights in that book I read."

Elizabeth paused for a moment and then looked John straight in the face. "I almost forgot. What were you going to tell me about those warrants? How do you know they will serve arrest warrants on the Kid and my father?"

"The sheriff filled me in on it. He said he'd gone to the district court to swear out warrants against the Kid and his men. Your father too. Judge Conroy signed off on them."

"The district court!"

"Yep. It was the only way to do it. We want to keep on the right side of the law in this fight. It had to be done."

Elizabeth looked at John with blazing eyes and said firmly, "That means you were involved in getting those warrants."

John was silent.

Anger rose in Elizabeth like a giant wave, threatening to overwhelm anything in its path. "You dirty scoundrel! You've been standing here telling me you love me, yet you were holding back that you were involved in these arrest warrants being issued. Including the one for my father!"

John was in deep water, maybe too deep, and he pleaded with her, "Elizabeth, there's still time to get this mess straightened out. Talk your father into breaking away from the Kid. Take me to him, and we can work out a deal to end this war right now."

Elizabeth turned away from John. Tears were forming in her eyes, and she didn't want him to see them. She hastily brushed them away, furious that she had let this foolish cowboy bring her to such a state. She walked over to her horse, untied it, and scurried into the saddle. She turned the horse back to face John.

She spoke in an even voice, venom dripping from every word. "My father will never run the Kid off the Flying C. He's loyal to his friends and the men he hires. He doesn't tell a girl how much he loves her while knowing he'll stab her in the back. I'm going to help my father in this war. When you count your enemies in this valley, include me. I ride for the Flying C and no one else."

Elizabeth spurred her horse, and it jumped forward before taking off. She passed John, and as she did, she swung a heavy leather riding quirt at him. He didn't have time to dodge, but reflexively flinched, covering his face. A sharp sting crossed the back of his shoulders. It hurt. Elizabeth was strong and struck the blow as hard as she could. He was sure she left a considerable mark, but it wasn't as bad as the sickness he felt in his stomach.

She was gone before he could even straighten himself, and John was suddenly alone at their meeting spot. The only sound was the wind blowing through the trees.

THE LAW

*N*ews that warrants had been issued for the Stipic Kid, his men, and Branson Calloway spread in the valley like a wildfire. Sheriff Johnson saw no need to keep things a secret once he saw he had to act and, in a true political fashion, believed advancing his part in the matter would improve his position. His loud boasting about his intent to serve the warrants masked his real weakness of character and fear in carrying out the task. He'd swung from his normal state of indifference and laziness to one of exaggerated zeal.

Shortly after the judge signed the warrants, John Colberg was in Boulder Valley getting supplies when he came upon the sheriff talking to a small group of people. Sheriff Johnson told the group he intended to serve the arrest warrants at the Flying C alone the next day. John, astonished at hearing this, quickly interjected.

"Sheriff. For crying out loud, you don't want to undertake that task alone! It's suicide if you attempt to serve those arrest warrants yourself."

Johnson looked at Colberg with disdain and said, "Oh, it's you. Hello, Colberg. As you well know, I'm the law in this area. The citizens count on me to uphold it. It's a lonely, dangerous job, but I'm up to the task. What would these fine people think of me if I neglected my duty? In troubled times, a lawman must rise to the occasion."

John felt a mix of amusement and horror at Johnson's posturing. He said to him respectfully, "I'm not asking you to neglect your duty, Sheriff Johnson. I'd like you to accept the help of some of my armed cowboys. It couldn't hurt."

Johnson stood up straight and puffed out his chest. "Nope. I'll do it myself. I don't need help from the citizens to do my duties."

Fearful of the disaster ahead if the sheriff

attempted to serve the warrants alone, John rode to the Flying C. He implored Elizabeth to talk her father into declaring a truce in the cattle war and forestall further bloodshed. That attempt not only met with failure, but Elizabeth ran John off the Flying C under threat of violence.

As he rode back to the Two Dot, what bothered him the most was his belief that he had extinguished any chance he had with her. He was in love with her, plain and simple, and the sting of her riding quirt didn't change those feelings. Nor did the newfound anger and contempt she directed at him. He felt no bitterness toward her for being run off the Flying C. Just seeing her had been worth the risk. However, in retrospect, he knew it had been a foolish thing to do. He was lucky to be alive. Neither the Kid nor Branson had been around.

John's belief that he had blown it with Elizabeth generated the only hurt he felt, the pain that came from the possibility of not having more meetings with her. He was also angry with himself for falling so hard for someone who wouldn't reciprocate those feelings. Still, he knew he'd go to the Flying C again if an opportunity presented itself, whatever the consequences. However, John Colberg had little opportunity to dwell on his thoughts, as many events followed Sheriff Johnson's aborted attempt to serve the warrants.

* * *

WHEN THE STIPIC KID gave Branson notice of the arrest warrants, Branson laughed and waved his hand in dismissal. "Let the sheriff try to serve those warrants. I can go to court and prove every horn and hoof on this ranch. I have the money to bond out any Flying C man who gets arrested, including myself. There'll be hell to pay if I'm arrested. I can assure you of that."

The Kid didn't see things the same way. Arrest warrants meant jail, and jail possibly meant a brand of justice the Kid wanted to avoid. He knew his reputation in the territory and that most folks weren't likely to wait around for a trial. Once in jail, the Kid was helpless and firmly believed the public would lynch him. He didn't trust the legal system. Other men might look at the legal machinery as something they could bend or manipulate, but the Kid's crimes were many and infamous. He felt that most folks would be itching to see him swinging from a tree if he were ever captured; they wouldn't wait around for the law to run its course.

The more the Kid thought about his situation, the more he became convinced he couldn't allow the arrest warrants to be served. Branson Calloway was determined to twist the law to his advantage. He fought with the cunning of a fox and had the money and power to take that route. The Kid realized he had only one strategy that would work for him. He had to take matters into his own hands boldly and do it quickly.

THE KID LEARNED, through the grapevine, the day the warrants were to be served. On that day, the Stipic Kid gathered his men at the Flying C. He told them a good bit of excitement was coming and to be ready for it. The Kid knew his men were behind him entirely. After all, they were all in the same boat; if the Kid swung from a rope, his men would surely swing too. They'd been with the Kid through many illegal adventures and were criminals at heart. The Kid was only their superior in the quickness he carried in his gun hand and the nonchalant attitude with which he carried out his criminal enterprises.

Riding to Boulder Valley by a circular route, the Kid and his men hid in the stockyards on the edge of town. They knew the sheriff would have to pass the area on his way out of town to the Flying C.

As they waited, the Kid whispered to the men, "That no good sheriff must go. If you let him by you and he gets to the Flying C, you boys are as good as hung."

As the Kid's men waited, passing a bottle of whiskey, John Colberg was on his way from the Two Dot with a group of his cowboys. He intended to provide Johnson with a strong guard, whether he liked it or not. John realized the sheriff's loose lips and brashness about his intention to serve the warrants alone had most likely alerted the Kid. That meant serious trouble for the sheriff if he didn't have enough men to make resistance unpalatable. John received word that Johnson would serve the warrants that day, and he wanted to arrive in Boulder Valley with his men before the sheriff started on his journey.

* * *

SHERIFF JOHNSON WAS READY, and called out to his deputy, "Mathew, get the horses. It's time to head to the Flying C."

Mathew dutifully left the small building that served as a jail and Boulder Valley Sheriff's Office, and headed to the livery stable where the horses were kept when the lawmen didn't immediately need them. Inside his office, Johnson took a last drink of strong coffee, rose from his chair, and prepared himself for the task ahead.

When the deputy returned with the horses, both men mounted up slowly and headed out of town. They rode at a leisurely pace, and only Mathew showed any tension in his body.

Johnson took note of his deputy's distressed state and said, "It sure is a fine day, Mathew. Once we get this job done, it will be even nicer. Are you nervous?"

Mathew nodded stiffly. "A little. I think

any man would be nervous when they might face the Stipic Kid."

Johnson tried to calm the young man. "Don't worry about it. If I understand the situation correctly, Calloway won't let the Kid do anything to us. He is the type of man who likes to bend the law to do his bidding. I'm sure he is figuring on using the law to get out of this situation. Hell, we might even have to switch back to his side if the wind blows that way. He wouldn't dare let the Kid harm a hair on our heads. It doesn't serve his purposes. What we're doing today is no more dangerous than going to a Sunday picnic."

Mathew wasn't convinced. "Boy, I sure hope so, Sheriff. We're traveling a little light to be going up against the Kid."

Johnson smiled at his deputy and said in a fatherly tone, "Don't worry, young man. I have everything figured out."

The lawmen rode on in silence until they reached the edge of the corrals at the stockyards.

As they neared the spot where the Kid and his men were waiting, the Kid hissed, "I get the first shot. Nobody else fires. I want the sheriff for myself."

A shot rang out. Johnson fell backward in his saddle and his horse reared. He then tumbled to the ground with a heavy thud as his horse whirled about, galloping back toward the center of the town. Mathew was stunned at what had happened. He frantically looked around for the origin of the shot. The Kid's men fired at the deputy, and he slumped forward. His horse took off at a gallop past the shooting men, bullets whizzing about it. After a short distance, Mathew fell from the saddle. The horse, relieved of its rider, turned around and raced back toward its companion. Neither man moved as they lay in the street. The sheriff lay on his back with his arms outstretched. The deputy was on his side, curled up.

A momentary silence settled over the scene before the assassins mounted their horses. Then, they rode into the street with guns drawn, looking for anyone who might challenge them. Convinced no one would take them on, the Kid rode up to Johnson's still body.

He looked down in disgust and sneered, "That will teach you to serve warrants on the likes of me, lawman." The outlaw drew his pistol, firing the remaining rounds into the dead man as a last insult.

The Kid and his men spurred their horses and took off from Boulder Valley toward the Flying C, whooping and hollering. As they left town, John Colberg and his men arrived. Informed of the situation, they took off in hot pursuit of the Kid's gang. The bodies of the slain lawmen remained in the street until a group of citizens gathered them. They took the corpses to the local undertaker, who also ran the town's butcher shop.

THE CABIN

*T*he Stipic Kid always rode a fast horse, so did his men. They believed speed alone would determine the outcome if a posse tried to run them down and didn't think beyond that in their choice of mounts. However, no one had pursued the Kid in earnest because of his fearsome reputation. Not really. Most attempts were chiefly for show, or the Kid sniffed out the situation in advance and left before anyone could get on his trail. But this time he faced a different foe. One determined to get him at all costs.

John Colberg and the Two Dot cowboys rode Cayuse ponies, a horse uniquely suited for the territory they lived in. The ponies combined hardiness with both speed and endurance, an ideal combination of traits for the territory in which the animals worked.

And so, the chase was on, both pursuer and pursued believing they held the upper hand. The advantage goes to the one doing the chasing in a pursuit on horseback, and Colberg saw the Kid's group's dust cloud in the distance. He urged his men to press the chase to the limit.

* * *

THE KID's horse began to tire, and it didn't take long for him to realize he couldn't make it to the Flying C before his adversary ran him down.

He yelled to his men, "We won't make it to the Flying C! There's an old cabin in those trees ahead where we can make a stand and give them hell. Ride for it hard."

The Kid and his gang whipped their horses, sending them galloping through the trees, dodging and jumping obstacles. The animals were exhausted by the time they arrived at the cabin, but the men didn't pause to rest. Without wasting a second, they scram-

bled off their mounts and tied the horses behind the building. Each man then quickly
fanned out around the dwelling, trying to
find defensive positions. Despite its dilapidated condition, the logs of the cabin provided some protection around the door and
windows. The thick forest that surrounded it
gave plenty of cover and reduced visibility for
both attacker and defender.

The Kid moved among his men, eyes lit up
with excitement and anger. But an astute observer would've seen a little fear in those
eyes, too.

The Kid peered into the trees, eyes darting
back and forth. "Remember, boys. Don't
waste your ammunition. Wait until they get
close, and you can see them. Make good
shots. We can turn this thing around and get
back to the Flying C. Don't panic.

"Let me get the shot at Colberg. Understand? He's mine. I want to make him suffer.
You boys can have Foust and any of the
others with him."

* * *

JOHN COLBERG WATCHED as the Kid and his gang dove off the path and crashed through the trees. He knew a cabin was in the dense forest, and if the Kid had any sense, he'd be setting up an ambush or preparing for a siege. There was no going back now—it was time to face the Kid, and John's men were looking to him for guidance. He paused, deep in thought, when suddenly, Odie Foust galloped up on his horse and skidded to a halt in front of him, kicking up clouds of dust around them both. John stared at the woods, trying to decide what to do next.

He looked over at Odie and pointed to the forest. "Odie. There's a cabin in those trees, and the Kid can make a pretty good show of it against us. If we rush in there, we'll likely lose some people. I don't want that to happen. I think I have a plan to surround the Kid and keep our risk at a minimum."

Odie pushed his hat back on his head. "Well, let's hear it. I could do without a bullet in me today."

John sighed and began, "The Kid has a good spot, but in his rush, he may not consider that the cabin backs up to a small hill in those trees. We can use that to our advantage.

We'll send some men in there to confront them directly. Those men will stay as safe as possible behind cover and draw the fire of the Kid's men. Keep them distracted. You'll lead those men."

Foust nodded. "OK. What's next?"

"I'll take some men and sneak up the back of the hill. We'll come down on top of the Kid or to his side and catch him off guard. Hopefully, he'll be so surprised he'll surrender. If not, we'll have the drop on the lot of them if it comes to a shootout."

Odie mulled the plan over and wasn't quite convinced it would work. "Hmm. That sounds pretty good, John. But what makes you think the Kid hasn't planned on you trying to come in behind him?"

"The Kid is under pressure. Probably more pressure than anyone has put on him. If we keep him focused on the people in front of him, I'm betting on him not thinking about much else. Surrounding him is the best chance we've got, and that's what we're going to do."

Odie shrugged his shoulders and said, "Sounds good to me."

John Colberg was ready for action. He

sat up straight in the saddle, stating reso-
lutely, "Alright. Let's get our parties formed
up and get this thing going. I sure as hell
don't want this situation to continue after
dark."

The two parties were formed, and Colberg's group set off for their destination at a
determined pace. Odie watched as they disappeared into the tree line, their shapes
melting among the trees until they were gone
from sight. He felt a pang of hesitation as he
gathered the remaining men around him, but
it passed quickly. There was work to do and
it was time to do it.

"OK, gentlemen. Head up the trail and
ride hard to where the Kid entered the trees.
We want him to know we're coming."

The horses galloped along, the riders
pushing them forward. Their hooves
pounded against the ground, and the sound
echoed into the forest. The group pulled up
sharply at the edge of the trees, and in one
fluid motion, the riders slid off their mounts,
tying them to nearby branches. Those with
rifles pulled them out of scabbards, loading
rounds into chambers with a methodical
click-clack. Odie's face was tight as he stared

into the shadowed depths of the forest, then he turned to face his men.

He scanned the cowboys around him, looking for weakness or lack of resolve, and saw none. He smiled and said in a slow drawl, "Is everybody ready? Let's go. Don't be afraid to make some noise. We want the Kid focused solely on us."

As Odie moved forward, he waved his arms in front of him. "Spread out some. Keep yourselves covered. We don't know exactly where they are. Find a good spot and lie low when you get close to the cabin and can make it out. Don't take any risks. If this plan works out, we'll catch the Kid with nobody getting hurt on our side. Let me do the talking. Does everybody understand?"

The men nodded and spread out as they slowly entered the trees. Odie did the same and went out of his way to make noise. He deliberately stepped on small sticks and rushed through the brush toward the cabin. He could tell the men were following his instructions, as there was noise on either side of him.

He whispered to himself, "The Kid is likely to know we're here now."

* * *

THE KID STOOD in the dilapidated cabin's doorway when he heard noises in the forest. His head perked up immediately, and his ears turned toward the sounds like a dog's might do. He grinned. In that moment he recognized the source of the sound, and knew his adversaries were coming. He was ready for it.

He shouted to his men, "They're coming. I can hear them. Get ready. And try not to get shot. This is no time to be stupid. Keep your wits about you and we'll do these fools in. Don't forget. Colberg is mine."

The Kid's men readied their guns and waited. The day would bring a fight, there was no way around it, and they didn't want to lose.

* * *

JOHN COLBERG INCHED FORWARD on his hands and knees, sweat soaking through his shirt from the exertion. He peered cautiously into the abyss of darkness below him, listening for the telltale sounds of movement in the forest. He knew the cabin was somewhere down there, somewhere hidden among the trees, but the foliage was too thick to see anything. Looking back over his shoulder, he saw his men, their faces gaunt with anticipation. He put a finger to his lips, then waved them forward.

He addressed them in a whisper. "Listen up. We'll move down this slope quietly and take up positions on either side of the cabin. Get to a spot that puts you a bit in front. Stay away from the cabin. There will likely be men in front of the building, but I'm guessing they'll stay close to it. Also, if Odie did his job, the Kid's gang will be focused on what is in front of them.

"Don't shoot until I make my move. I don't care what anybody else is doing. I am going to try to get the Kid to surrender. We must maintain the element of surprise. If you see any of the Kid's men, get a bead on them. Be ready to shoot if the Kid doesn't give up."

John and his men made their way down the slope stealthily. They took up their positions and waited. No one, friend or foe, knew of their close presence.

* * *

ODIE CROUCHED BEHIND A TOWERING PINE, the thick trunk providing cover from any bullets that might come his way. He inhaled deeply, trying to steady his nerves, and peered around the edge of the tree. In the distance, he could make out the outline of the cabin. An unnatural stillness filled the air; even the birds had gone quiet. The Kid's men were there, no doubt about it. He could detect their movements in front of the building as they nervously changed positions. It was now or never.

Odie stood up and turned around, resting his back against the tree. He pointed his rifle at the ground and spoke loudly. "Hey, Kid! We got you surrounded. Tell your men to throw down their guns, and nobody will get hurt. I give you my word."

The Kid's reply came quickly. "Is that you, Foust? I wouldn't give you a bucket of piss for your word. Are you doing the talkin' for the Two Dot now? Where's Colberg? Too chicken to face me one-on-one."

"Don't worry. John's here. Why don't you just surrender? Save us all a bunch of trouble. You're not getting out of this scrape, Kid."

As soon as Odie quit speaking, someone

fired a shot. It was unclear who discharged their weapon, but the effect was immediate. A gunfight broke out, with all combatants shooting in each other's general direction. The forest's thickness and the distance between the men ruled out the possibility of precision. The wild gunfire hit no one. The shooting went on for some time, then died out as suddenly as it had started.

* * *

NEITHER JOHN nor his men had fired a shot. They all maintained discipline, and took the opportunity afforded by the gunfight to move closer to the cabin.

John cautiously took his position behind a fallen tree, its trunk providing ample cover. He set his rifle on top of it, using the makeshift barricade to steady his weapon. His eyes narrowed as he scanned the forest, focusing on any shape that might reveal one of the Kid's men. Suddenly, a ray of sunlight glinted off a metal buckle, catching his eye. The silhouette of one of the Kid's men revealed itself in the hazy light. John stilled his breathing and locked on to his target. It wasn't yet time to fire. He needed to talk to the Kid first.

John called out, "Kid, this is Colberg. The game is up. Surrender now. Don't be a fool. We have the drop on you. Don't sacrifice men for nothing."

The Kid realized John's voice came from the cabin's side and not in front. He leaned out of the cabin's doorway and took a shot in the direction of the voice, then ducked back inside.

The action precipitated another gunfight, but this time the consequences were deadly. John's group joined the fray and quickly felled two of the Kid's men. Another screamed out in pain.

The Kid knew he was in trouble. He also figured there might be another way out of the predicament if he surrendered. His mind raced.

Calloway might use his power with the law to free me. I can always break out of jail. It can't be that hard around here. That's if a lynch mob doesn't get me. No. Colberg is a law-and-order man. He won't let them lynch me. Besides, the people in Boulder Valley are too scared of me to attempt it. Yep. It's time to call it quits. Live to fight another day.

The Kid yelled out, "Stop shooting! Stop shooting, boys!"

The gunfire slowly died out, and silence again took over the forest. The Kid hesitated, a lingering doubt about surrendering still swirling in his mind. Then the moment of doubt passed. Giving himself up was the best course of action.

The Kid called out, "Alright, Colberg. I'm giving up. Men, do you hear me? We're giving up—no more shooting. Colberg, make sure that dirty dog Odie Foust doesn't shoot me down in cold blood. Do I have your assurance no one will shoot us if we surrender and throw down our guns?"

John's voice came from the forest, "You have my word. Gather in front of the cabin. Put your guns on the ground and your hands in the air. Move quickly."

The Kid stepped out of the cabin and stood a few feet in front of it. He undid his gun belt and dropped it on the ground. He raised his hands and glanced from side to side, searching for his men. They emerged from the forest and gathered around him, dropping their weapons. Even the wounded man joined the group, having suffered only a flesh wound to his shoulder. Two, however, did not appear.

The Kid shook his head in apparent sadness and said, "They got Georgie and Pete. I've ridden with them for quite a while. Oh well, that's the nature of this life. Don't worry, gents. We'll find a way out of this situation. I guarantee it."

Again, John called out from the forest, "Is that everybody?"

"Yep. That's the lot of us, Colberg."

"It better be, Kid. OK, men. Come out and keep your guns on them."

John and his men materialized, weapons drawn and aimed at their enemies. Odie and the others joined them. John approached the Kid and looked him over from head to toe. He never could reconcile the danger the Kid posed with the way he looked; his appearance didn't warn of danger at all.

John shook his head and said, "Dang, Kid. I must say, I'm a bit surprised at capturing you. I guess I was lucky today."

John pointed to the pile of guns on the ground. "Boys, gather these guns, retrieve the horses, and get these men tied up. Tie them so they can ride but not make a run for it. We must get them back to Boulder Valley; justice will soon run its course."

The Kid and his men were silent as the tasks to secure them were completed. For their part, John and the Two Dot cowboys didn't boast or mock their captured foes, and the atmosphere remained subdued. Everyone felt deep fatigue.

The men helped the captives onto their horses and guarded them. They retrieved the two dead outlaws and secured them across saddles. The horses carrying the deceased didn't protest their ghoulish cargo, and the group was on its way to Boulder Valley in no time.

* * *

CAPTORS AND CAPTIVES rode at a relaxed pace. Thoughts concerning the Kid's security in the Boulder Valley jail and Branson Calloway occupied John's mind. It wouldn't take long for Calloway to learn of the capture of the Kid and his men. Then what? How would they get Calloway into custody? He still had plenty of men at the Flying C, and he'd hole up there and fight. If they successfully apprehended Calloway, what would be his fate? How would Elizabeth react? What would happen to her?

The Kid rode between Colberg and Foust, looking down and appearing to be deep in thought. Suddenly, Foust turned to him and said, "How did you come to be called the Stipic Kid?"

The Kid's head jerked up. He looked at Odie Foust in surprise, then straight ahead, thinking for a moment.

"I was raised in the eastern part of the territory near a place called Deer Creek. It was close to a big river. We had a small ranch where my folks barely scraped out a living. Most folks didn't have much. Only a few rich ranchers had anything.

"North of Deer Creek was a large ranch called the Stipic Ranch. There wasn't anybody by the name of Stipic on it. I don't know why the hell they called it that. Anyway, people called Charboneau ran the place. Folks around the area said they came from up north, but I don't know."

The Kid paused, still perplexed by the fact

that the Stipic Ranch had no one by that name living on it. It never did seem right to him.

Then he continued, speaking in a relaxed manner, "I worked at the place when I was real young. We needed the money, and sometimes they paid in vittles, which was more valuable to us. One Charboneau man was the cook, and he was terrible. On top of it, he was also a mean character. I tired of him, so one day, I shot him."

The Kid smiled at the memory of shooting Charboneau.

"The Charboneau folks didn't take kindly to me shooting one of their own, so I hit the outlaw trail quick. I've been on it ever since. After the shooting, people started calling me the Stipic Kid, and I guess it stuck."

Foust let out a hearty laugh. "Good grief, Kid. Cooks sure don't fare too well around you."

The Kid shrugged. "I'm particular about my meals. A bad cook puts me in a sour mood, and a grumpy one turns me even darker. It just ain't right. A man should get a decent meal in this world. Especially if he's working hard."

Foust laughed even harder. "The Flying C must have one helluva cook. I haven't heard any news about you shooting the cook on that outfit."

"Well, the cook on the Flying C is a woman, and she's decent enough. I'm not in the habit of shooting women. It goes against my code."

John joined in the conversation. "That's true enough. I haven't heard of you shooting any women or children. I suspect it's only a matter of time. You don't seem to discriminate much with killin'."

The Kid snorted, offended that anyone would think he would shoot women or children. "I have some decency, Colberg. My mother was a fine cook. There used to be a strange fish in the big river. We'd catch one every once in a while. It had a long bill on it. Kind of like a duck's bill, but longer. I don't know how to describe it. My mother called them paddlefish. It was good eatin', and she would fry it up in the pan. She'd coat it in flour."

Foust threw a hand up in disbelief, causing his horse to flinch. "You should've gone into the storytelling business, Kid. It probably wouldn't pay as well as the outlaw business, but at least you might've come to a better end. I think I've heard everything now. A fish with a duck's bill. That's just plain crazy."

The Kid sneered at Odie. "That fish is as real as me sitting on this horse, Foust. As real as the bullet I plan to put in you someday."

Odie grinned. "Good luck with that. It'll have to be in the next life, although I think we're headed to different places. You'll have a date with a rope soon enough."

The Kid looked at John and said, "Hey, Colberg. Let's stop at those hot waters around here and take a soak before we get to town. Relax a little. I heard those waters cure just about anything that ails a person."

John replied darkly, "I doubt those waters will cure the ailment you're about to have."

The Kid smiled. The men quieted, and the rest of the ride to Boulder Valley was in silence.

Hours later, the Kid and his gang shuffled into the Boulder Valley jail. They were placed under heavy guard, and local cowboys were pressed into service as jailers. Outside, a mob of angry locals had gathered, but none dared attempt anything for fear of John and his men, who threatened violent action if any vigilante justice were meted out. A local man, Ollinger, who had previous experience working as a lawman in the mining camps, was hastily sworn in as the new sheriff. Meanwhile, Branson Calloway was out there somewhere, and the entire valley waited for him to strike.

A VISIT

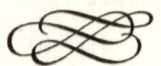

The night after the arrest of the Stipic Kid and his men, Elizabeth Calloway sought her father on the first floor of the sprawling ranch house. The main house at the Flying C was a large, formidable building constructed as a fortress. It loomed over the ranch compound and dominated it. Branson believed it to be impregnable.

It had an inner courtyard surrounded by a rectangular building of two stories. The entire structure had walls of enormous thickness, impervious to bullets. The rooms on the second floor opened onto a continuous balcony protected by a solid parapet. A similar parapet ran the length of the veranda on the first floor and the roof. All window shutters were a sufficient thickness to impede bullets and contained shooting slits. The windows in the structure were large, and an adult could easily climb through them if necessary. Although Branson built the house for protection, it was also a place of rustic beauty, and all who saw it commented on that fact.

She found him in his office. The activity on the Flying C was frantic. No one had expected the current turn of events, and the sudden loss of control created a cloud of anxiety that hung heavily over the ranch.

When the news of the Kid's capture first reached Branson Calloway, his first inclination was to send out riders to bring in all cowboys to the ranch. Then, launch an attack on the jail in Boulder Valley.

Branson quickly erased that thought from his mind. His shrewd and calculating nature took over. No, he couldn't attack the jail and succeed in the long run. The public would view a concerted attack on the jail as open defiance of the law. There was no way to predict where that would lead. Attempting it involved too much risk. Yes, Sheriff Johnson had double-crossed him, but he had paid with his life, his deputy, too. Branson reasoned that John Colberg and the rest of the valley must be in just as much turmoil as those on the Flying C. There was no need to act rashly.

Calloway thought he was safe from any warrants being served on him for the time being. Sure, a temporary sheriff had been appointed, but Branson felt if he could force an election for a new sheriff, he might turn the situation back in his favor. Calloway decided to see that an election took place. He would work hard to ensure that any new sheriff would be a dyed-in-the-wool Flying C man. As far as the Kid and his men were concerned, well, they were expendable. People like the Kid existed all over the frontier, and Branson could quickly find another gunman. He would sacrifice the Kid if necessary.

His confidence growing, Branson bragged to his daughter after she entered the office, "I'll get the man I want for sheriff even if I have to have an armed man at every voting station in the valley."

Elizabeth didn't share her father's enthusiasm for the election scheme. "But, Dad, they've already appointed a new man. What makes you think you can do that? It's open war in the valley, and things are turning against us. Are you sure you have enough protection? Maybe you should start carrying a gun."

Branson put his arm around his daughter's shoulders and gently squeezed. "Don't worry about me, Elizabeth. This isn't my first cattle war. Every war has its trials. I never had to carry a firearm in any of them. I have plenty of hired guns around here. It's always better to pay people to do the shooting for you. Stay out of the messy part. Besides, I guard this ranch so well no one can get within range to even take a shot in my direction."

Still unconvinced, Elizabeth spoke with trepidation. "Things seem different this time. I never thought they'd get a hold of the Kid. To me, that's a bad omen. That no-good John Colberg is tenacious, like a starving dog who just got a taste of meat."

"Let me do the worrying, Elizabeth. Everything will work out in the end. Trust me."

Elizabeth moved to the open window in the room and looked out at the valley's beauty bathed in moonlight. The cool breeze coming through the open window felt good on her skin. The mountains in the distance, green and brown during the day, were dense and black. Monsters, waiting to pounce. Though the sky was full of bright stars, it provided her with none of the usual wonder and comfort. The valley's beauty was cold and menacing.

From the bunkhouse close to the house, Elizabeth heard guitar music and the men singing. It seemed impossible to her that such a beautiful place could now be associated with such trouble. She wore a simple dress, set off by a lace shawl wrapped around her shoulders. The only extravagance in her appearance was a necklace with a large, bright ruby. Her hair was down, and it stirred in the soft breeze.

Branson stared at her for a few moments. "Goodness, daughter. You remind me so much of your mother right now it hurts. You sure have become a beautiful woman, just like her."

Elizabeth's eyes glistened with tears. "Do you really think so? I haven't heard you mention her in a long time. Don't you think she'd want more for me now than I have?"

Branson frowned. "What do you mean? I provide for all your needs and then some. I let you do what you want. You have the best of everything. Horses. Clothes. Whatever you want. Someday, you'll be the owner of the largest ranch in this territory. You'll be able to ride all day and never leave your property."

Elizabeth became frustrated, and she stomped a foot on the floor like an angry child. "That's not what I'm talking about. I haven't been brought up like other young women. Like my mother. She was a lady."

Branson looked at her, perplexed.

She rolled her eyes and continued, "You don't understand, do you? I haven't received enough schooling. My education doesn't make it possible for me to be around upscale society. I don't know how to act around people like that. I just know how to rummage around in a wild country with rough people. That's not right. Mother wouldn't have wanted this. She was educated and sophisticated. I want to be that way, too."

Branson ran his hand through his hair. As he looked at Elizabeth, he no longer saw his daughter. He saw another young woman, one he'd known many years ago. A young mother who had plans for their child and how that child would be raised. It hit him like a punch to the gut, and his hands trembled. A mist came to his eyes. He realized he hadn't carried out her wishes at all. He'd only been concerned with his plans of conquest and had raised Elizabeth to help carry out those plans. He had never thought about anything else. He realized he'd failed his beloved wife and daughter by not considering their dreams, and in that moment, it hurt.

Branson looked at the floor and said softly, "You're right, Elizabeth. I thought I was doing right by you, making you tough. Making it so you could handle livin' in these places and make a go of it. Run a cattle empire. I was wrong. Just plain wrong."

"Dad, it's not enough that I know how to rope, ride, run a ranch, and how to deal with people like the Stipic Kid. There's got to be more to life than that."

Branson's revelation left him just as suddenly as it had arrived, and his general distrust of people pushed another thought into his head. This wasn't like his daughter at all; something wasn't right.

He looked at her with suspicion and spoke

forcefully. "Who's putting these ideas in your head? I haven't known you to hang around with any of the young women around here. Besides, none of them are educated society girls. Most of them are happy if they can go to a country dance occasionally. You were young when your mother passed away, so she couldn't have done it."

Elizabeth replied with disgust, "You're right. I don't have any female friends around here. As far as my mother goes, I know what she was. Why wouldn't she want the same for me? Do you think she would've wanted me to hang around a bunch of rough men all the time and adopt their ways? Do you think she would've wanted my entire life to re-volve around your cattle empire schemes? You don't have to worry. I won't turn against you. You can put that in the bank. I'm just starting to see things differently now."

Branson softened again but was still leery of his daughter's new ideas. "I guess you're right. Your mother would've wanted some-thing different for you. But what do you mean? Are you talking about going to a fin-ishing school for ladies? Something like that?

There might be one in Helena. I can have someone check into it."

"Yes, if it's possible. If not, you could bring in a tutor to further my education and teach me the ways of a lady. That way, I can be as much like my mother as possible. I'll still ride, rope, and work cattle. I can do both. Why do I have to put limits on what I can be? Why can't it be my choice?"

Branson thought about it and nodded in agreement. "From now on, the choice is yours. Do you want to start with your education right away?"

Elizabeth smiled and said, "No. Not right away. We have a cattle war to deal with. I still ride for the Flying C and want to see you done with this mess. When this war is settled, we will see about the schooling."

His daughter's loyalty moved Branson. He went over to her and gave her a long hug. Both stood at the open window, looking into the night. Suddenly, the sound of footsteps startled them, and Elizabeth instinctively moved in front of her father to shield him.

A low voice called out from the darkness, "Don't be afraid. I just want to talk. No harm will come to anyone. There is no need for shootin'."

John Colberg appeared at the open window. He jumped over the low window ledge into the room.

Both Elizabeth and her father stared at John with astonishment. He stood before them, smiling like a young boy filled with the pride of having successfully pulled off a prank.

"I passed on going through the front door. It seemed like a bad idea. The chances of me getting shot being high. I snuck around the house and saw you two standing in this room. So, here I am."

Branson blurted out, "How did you get here at all? My men are falling down on the job, that's for sure."

John was nonplussed and said matter-of-factly, "All places have weak spots. I have a quiet horse, and I'm stealthy myself. I passed right by all the trouble spots."

Branson looked at him coldly and said, "Well, now that you're here, what do you want?"

John glanced at Elizabeth and winked. He thought he'd never seen a more beautiful woman. She still hadn't recovered from his appearance, and her cheeks were flushed, eyes wide with surprise.

He looked back at Branson. "I want to talk to you about something important. Important enough that I'm willing to risk my life for it. That's why I took this chance and came here tonight."

Branson laughed, still taken aback at the young man's brashness. But a small part of him admired the boldness of the Two Dot owner.

"You sure as hell did take a chance, coming here like this. You'd be done if I called out to my men now. That's for sure, Colberg. They'd put an end to you right quick."

"I agree with you, Calloway. They wouldn't have much trouble. I'm unarmed. But I'm bettin' you're not gonna call them."

"Assuming I won't call them. What is it you want, cowpuncher?"

John Colberg took on the manner of a diplomat. Standing erect and dignified, he said, "I want to talk to you about this cattle war. It must stop. Nobody is going to win, and that includes you. Let's come to an agreement of some sort to end this craziness."

Branson was having none of it, and he replied with determination, "My mind's made up. I'm going to see this thing through. I'm going to run my affairs as I see fit, and no cowpuncher is going to change that. Everything I've done has been legal. It's been proven in the courts."

"Yet, Calloway, the courts have issued warrants for the arrest of you and your men. You aren't operating on the right side of the law anymore."

Branson's voice rose in protest. "Those warrants were obtained through pure trickery. Now, look what's happened. Sheriff Johnson and his deputy are both dead. I lay that at your feet."

John discarded diplomacy and pointed a finger at Branson. "You're outside of the law, Calloway! You just can't see it. Stop before it's too late."

Branson yelled at him, "I'm not outside of the actual law. Just the fake law you drummed up. I don't recognize your fabricated law. I'm going to fight it!"

John was exasperated. How could Calloway be so thick-headed? His exasperation now caused him to take the conversation in an entirely new direction, a dangerous new direction.

"You have more to consider than yourself, Calloway. Your daughter relies on you. You must consider her situation."

Branson's face tightened. "What the hell is my daughter to you?"

John looked at the floor for a moment, then looked Branson straight in the eye. "She's everything to me."

The statement astounded Branson. "For the love of God! How can this be? I've got a mind to call my men right now and have you strung up."

Branson looked from John to Elizabeth and then back again, studying them closely.

The truth of the matter struck him like a thunderbolt. "I'll be! I believe you are in love with her! That won't do you much good, though. Elizabeth won't take up with you against me. She rides for the Flying C. Isn't that right, Elizabeth?"

Elizabeth whispered, hesitation in her voice, "No, Dad ... I won't go against you."

Branson was enraged, his body tensed, and he shouted, "What? That's not exactly a ringing endorsement. I think this fool has been putting all these crazy ideas in your head. He's been telling you I'm not raising you right. Are you in love with him?"

Elizabeth responded, anger in her voice, "No. I'm not in love with him. I thought I was, but he turned out to be a low-down scoundrel. I won't love anyone who crosses you or the Flying C."

Branson smiled triumphantly and said, "That's my girl. What do you think of that, Mr. Colberg? Elizabeth rides for the Flying C brand."

John grimaced. Elizabeth's declaration hurt him, like she'd stabbed him. Still, it didn't change his feelings. He still wanted her, but he put that aside. There was business that needed to be straightened out.

John tried one more time to get Branson to change his mind. "Calloway, you must see reason. If not, this will be a long war. The Two Dot will fight you to the bitter end. How much does one man need? Where does it stop? You're flat-out wrong. Elizabeth will pay for it in the end."

Branson spoke calmly, confidently. "I'm willing to risk everything, young man. Elizabeth is too. That's the simple truth of it."

John threw his hands up, realizing he was wasting his time. There would be no more entreaties on his part, and he said with resignation, "So be it. At least grant me one concession. Let the law take care of the Stipic Kid. He's nothing more than a mad-dog killer, with no redeeming value. There's no changing someone like that. Let's both agree to be done with him. If you're a man of the law, as you claim, there's no need for such a man to be running around causing havoc."

Calloway laughed derisively. "What are you talking about? The Kid worked for your outfit at one time."

"That was before we knew him to be a cold-blooded killer. Once we found that out, Odie Foust and I swore to take care of him for good."

Calloway shrugged his shoulders. "He's in jail now, isn't he? It looks like his days are numbered."

"That's true. I'm asking you not to break him out of jail. Let the law take care of him. If the Flying C tries to break him out, the new sheriff has sworn to shoot the Kid at the first attack on the jail. He means business. You won't get the Kid and might lose some of your men, too."

Before Branson Calloway could answer, hoofbeats came from the darkness outside. Soon, several horsemen appeared out of the night, whooping and hollering. One voice stood out among all the commotion, yelling orders to the raucous men.

Branson's eyes widened. "That's the Kid! He broke out of jail. You're in a tough spot now. All your talk about letting the law take care of the Kid came to nothing."

Branson quickly stepped to his desk, opened a drawer, and removed a pistol. He laid the gun on the desk and motioned to Elizabeth.

"Be quick. Take this gun. It's the only one I own. Guard this cowpuncher while I go out and see what's going on with the Kid. He's animated right now and will be doubly dangerous."

John sat in a chair in the room's corner, away from the window. Elizabeth didn't pick up the pistol at first. She stared at John, and he stared back. Neither spoke. The silence seemed to last forever, but only a few moments passed. Then Elizabeth moved to the desk and picked up the gun. Her worry wasn't John Colberg, it was the possibility of running into the Kid or one of his men as she helped John escape.

She motioned to John and said in a low voice, "Come along, John. I'll take you out the back, away from the Kid. I hope we don't run into anybody."

Elizabeth moved to the door, and he followed without comment. They crept down a hallway and exited the house. Once outside, John pulled Elizabeth to him.

He whispered to her, "You do love me, don't you?"

Elizabeth wrestled herself free from his grasp, moving back a couple of steps.

She said icily, "No. I believe I might hate you more than I did when I hit you with that riding quirt. Your only salvation is that I wouldn't hand over my worst enemy to the Kid."

Then she was gone, returning to the house without even a glance at the stunned rancher. John silently retrieved his horse, left the Flying C in haste, and was soon beyond the reach of either Branson Calloway or the Kid.

JAILBREAK

Gary Ollinger grimaced as he thought about his new prisoner. From his viewpoint, he had been forced into duty as the sheriff, and Ollinger didn't relish his new role. Being responsible for the Stipic Kid and his men wasn't a job he wanted. His deputies, if you could call them that, were nothing more than cowboys with no training or experience in enforcing the law. Sure, they were game, but being game didn't cut it when dealing with a man like the Kid. Ollinger had given orders to always keep a standing guard over the Kid and his men, no exceptions.

The Kid's cell and that of his men were on the second floor of the jail. The lower level of the jail had an office area, a gun rack, and another cell, which usually contained a drunk needing to sleep off a wild time on the town. The building hadn't been designed to be a prison. It was originally a dry goods store with a living area on the second floor. The first owner left to seek his fortune elsewhere, and the building was reconstituted to serve its current purpose. The new dry goods purveyor in town had built his own store.

The Kid seemed disinterested in the entire affair. He didn't manifest the slightest emotion regarding his predicament. In fact, the Kid was so subdued during his incarceration that many guards believed he'd given up and accepted his fate.

The rumor of the Kid's attitude spread around town. Boulder Valley was small, and rumors spread quickly into every nook and cranny of the community. The Kid's capture had created a keen buzz among the towns-people, but now that buzz had dissipated. With the Kid seemingly subdued for good, a mood like the Kid's settled over the town. Where Boulder Valley had been teeming with armed men in its streets, now there were few. The idea that Branson Calloway would attempt to break the Kid out of jail seemed to have been abandoned by the residents.

The new sheriff didn't hold the same belief as the townspeople. He was still concerned about Calloway. Ollinger wanted John Colberg and his cowboys to help guard the Kid in case Branson Calloway attempted to free the outlaw. But after depositing the Kid and his men in jail, John had left Boulder Valley.

Before he swung into the saddle, John had tipped his hat to the crowd assembled outside the jail. The last thing he said to Ollinger before he rode off was, "Mark my words, if Calloway thinks you're ready to pull the trigger on the Kid at the slightest sign of trouble, he won't bother trying to bust him out. Make sure the word gets around that you mean business, and everything will be fine."

Ollinger wasn't convinced, and wanted to refute Colberg's statement but didn't have any evidence to do so. The sheriff decided the only way to ensure the Kid stayed put was to take no chances—chain him up by hand and foot in a cell and keep the key hidden.

* * *

ALTHOUGH IT SEEMED to the outside observer that the Kid had given up all hope, what wasn't seen or known was that he never stopped trying. His astute eyes had quickly assessed his situation after being locked in his cell. The Kid knew from experience that counting on someone else to help only ended in disappointment. He wasn't going to wait around for anybody, including Calloway. He needed to turn his predicament around. It didn't take long for him to put a plan into action.

As a guard was languishing sleepily in a chair, the Kid loudly exclaimed, "It sure looks like this is the end. I don't have a chance in the world now. Hey guard, could you show a little kindness and bum me some tobacco for a smoke?"

The guard lazily rose from the chair and approached the Kid. He gave him some tobacco and wrapping papers. After all, what could it hurt to show a little kindness to a doomed man? The Kid rolled his cigarette expertly and the guard lit it for him. He inhaled deeply, held it for a moment and then exhaled a cloud of smoke.

The Kid relaxed, feigning satisfaction.

"Yep. I sure stepped in it this time. I'm glad my mother isn't here to see what became of me. Dang. I'm gettin' mighty hungry. I haven't eaten in some time. Would it be possible to rustle up a little grub?"

The guard thought about it and replied, "Sure, Kid. I don't see why not. A man's got to eat sometime. I'll get you some food."

The guard marched away, determined to deliver the Kid's meal. As he passed by the cell containing the Kid's men, their desperate cries filled the air. "Get us food too!" and "We're starving!" they shouted. He continued unfazed. The men's rage was palpable and expressed as a series of curses hurled at their perceived tormentor.

The guard was nonplussed by the behavior and waved his hand at them. "If you men had shown me a little more respect, I might be inclined to feed you, too. As it stands, until you do, you'll all go hungry."

The guard cleared his errand with Ollinger and set off from the jail to the small hotel across the street. It was the only place in Boulder Valley that prepared food. In a short time, he returned with some soup and old bread. Sitting at his desk, Ollinger amused himself with a deck of cards. His rifle rested against the wall within reach should he need it.

The guard went up the stairs to deliver the food to the Kid. Ollinger set the deck of cards down. He was sleepy, and once the guard's footsteps reached the second floor, he pulled his hat over his face. What could a quick nap hurt? Everything was calm and under control.

The guard approached the Kid's cell with the food.

The Kid smiled and acted like he was breathing in the aroma of the meal. "Boy, that sure smells good. Thank you. But you'll have to put it through the bars if you can. I can't reach it with these restraints on me."

The guard moved forward and tried passing the food through the bars with one hand. In a flash, the Kid seized the guard's hand and pulled him close to the cell. The soup fell from the man's hand and splattered all over the floor. The guard was stunned at the Kid's grip strength. He also saw the hand holding him was free of restraints. The Kid had slipped one of his small hands through the manacles. His wrist was raw and bloody where he had forced it through the restraint, but his grasp didn't waver.

Murderous intent filled the Kid's eyes and he hissed, "Free me, or you'll die. If you yell or make a commotion, you'll die. Make the right choice. Take your keys and unlock the cell door."

The guard was terrified. He could've drawn his revolver, but his fear of the Kid paralyzed him from doing anything other than following the Kid's instructions. The guard meekly drew his keys from his pocket and unlocked the Kid's cell door. As soon as the lock clicked open, the outlaw thrust his still-manacled hand through the cell bars and relieved the guard of his pistol. The Kid stepped outside the cell, switched the pistol to his free hand and covered the guard with the weapon. The man slowly backed up with his hands in the air.

The Kid gestured to the guard. "Get yourself in that cell. If you make any quick moves, you'll be tasting lead."

The guard did as the outlaw instructed. As he moved past the Kid to enter the cell, the outlaw struck him in the back of the head with the manacled hand. The guard fell forward into the cell, stunned, dropping the keys on the floor just outside. The Kid retrieved the keys, closed the cell door, and locked it. He then freed his men. They hurried out of their cell, gathering around the Kid. The outlaw tried to unlock his restraints, but none of the keys fit.

The Kid spoke softly. "I told you I'd find a way out of this situation. The keys to unlock these chains aren't here. They must be downstairs.

"I'll sneak down there and take care of the situation. I hope I don't have to make too much noise, but if I do, that's just the way it goes. When I call you, come down quick and grab a gun. Cartridges, too, if you can get them. There must be plenty of horses tied up on the street. Everybody grabs one. Shoot whoever you need to and get to movin' out of this town quick. We'll circle up outside town on the trail to the Flying C. OK. Here we go."

The Kid tiptoed down the stairs. He still had chains on his legs and one arm. Walking was noisy and difficult. The Kid cursed his predicament; he didn't want to alert whoever was in the office. The outlaw thought it was probably only Ollinger. A smile crossed the

Kid's face. If Ollinger was still there, the Kid meant to ruin his day. While the rest of the jail staff usually went about their duties quietly and efficiently, the Kid had been taunted and cursed by the sheriff when placed in the jail. The sheriff had described the fate that awaited the outlaw in gruesome detail. Now, the bill had come due for his obnoxious behavior.

At the bottom of the stairs, the Kid peeked around the corner. He couldn't believe his luck. Ollinger was leaning back in his chair, hat pulled over his face, asleep. The outlaw barely repressed a laugh as he took careful aim and shot Ollinger in the head. Ollinger's body jerked instinctively, causing the chair to fall backward, depositing him on the floor in a heap.

The Kid moved to the closest window peering out onto Boulder Valley's main street. Nothing looked out of the ordinary. No one outside knew what was happening inside the jail. Still, the Kid thought things could turn against him quickly. He couldn't dally.

He called out, "Men! Get down here. I killed Ollinger. We don't have much time."

The men ran down the stairs, joining the

Kid in the office. The outlaw rummaged around, looking for the keys to his restraints, but he couldn't find them.

The Kid was incensed and shouted, "For crying out loud! I can't find those cursed keys anywhere! Time for a change of plans. The blacksmith is just a few buildings down the street. I need a man to go with me and help. The rest of you run into the street, grab a horse, and head out. Make a lot of noise. Scare the hell out of the fools. It'll keep the attention off me. Meet me in that stand of trees where the trail branches off to the Flying C. Get moving."

The men grabbed rifles and ammunition and headed into the street. Soon, shooting and yelling filled the air. The Kid motioned to his aide, and the two snuck out a back door and headed toward the blacksmith's shop. Their movement was comical, the Kid hopping forward with one arm around his companion, his companion keeping time with the Kid's tempo. Still, they moved faster than anyone would've thought possible.

The pair of outlaws entered the back of the blacksmith shop and approached the blacksmith, who had his back to them, absorbed in a task.

The Kid spoke firmly and loudly. "Put your hands up! Be quick about it."

The blacksmith, surprised, whirled around. Seeing two guns pointed at him, he threw his hands up.

The Kid said urgently, "Free me from these restraints. Don't waste time or I'll do you in. It makes no difference to me, smithy."

The blacksmith set about his task without comment. In no time, the Kid was free from the restraints.

The Kid turned to his companion. "Check out the front and see if any saddled horses are nearby. With all the commotion, there may not be."

The man went to the front of the shop and cautiously peered outside. He looked back at the Kid and said, "Yep. There's a couple of horses real close to this place, saddled and ready to go."

"Good. It's time to get the hell out of this godforsaken town. Thanks, smithy. Here's your payment."

The Kid shot the blacksmith in the leg, and he fell to the floor, writhing in pain.

The Kid laughed, amused at the blacksmith's contortions. "That should keep you from getting any crazy ideas. I reckon you can still do some smithing, even with a bum leg."

The Kid turned to his companion, motioned with his pistol, and said, "Let's go. Time's a wasting."

The two outlaws ran into the street, grabbed horses, and swiftly departed from Boulder Valley. Whooping and hollering as they left town, they shot at anybody who dared to show themselves. They faced no meaningful resistance and soon reached their rendezvous point. From there, the entire group headed out for the Flying C.

TROUBLES

The Kid's bold escape filled Branson Calloway with a newfound sense of optimism, banishing the dark thoughts that had threatened to overwhelm him. The doubts he held about his own parenting, and his capacity to outwit his new and relentless adversary, who also happened to be in love with his daughter, were pushed aside. He was left with only a fierce determination to succeed and conclude the cattle war on his terms. As the Kid strutted around the ranch, demanding whatever he pleased, Branson indulged his every whim. His own ambition was reflected back at him in the Kid's actions, and he felt victory was now within reach.

Elizabeth saw the Kid's growth in power and influence over her father, but she remained silent. She didn't remind her father of her desire for education or refinement, nor would she leave him until the cattle war concluded. She suffered in silence, hoping the outcome would favor the Flying C. However, deep inside, a part of her harbored worries for John Colberg. She would never admit it to anyone, least of all herself. But it was there, bubbling just under the surface, threatening to break free.

The valley had descended into a complete state of war. The killing of two sheriffs and a deputy created an environment bereft of official law and order. With the Stipic Kid free and undamaged, no one dared take on any law enforcement role. The legal apparatus of the area was completely paralyzed. Nothing would occur until the Flying C, or the Two Dot, prevailed in the ongoing war.

The Flying C took the fight to anyone who didn't support its cause. The Kid's gang even quickly showed the door to individuals who tried to stay neutral. Calloway took cattle with writs of attachment that he served himself, the Kid in tow. The Kid found Calloway's mock solemnity at serving writs hilarious and would burst out laughing at the farce.

Branson Calloway met resistance to his mock justice with violence. If Branson's henchmen didn't shoot down a resisting rancher immediately, they assassinated him later under cover of darkness. Many ranchers abandoned their places, either leaving the valley or moving to the Two Dot to join in opposing the Flying C.

The Flying C hadn't openly attacked the Two Dot yet. As such, the public viewed the ranch as the only safe place in the valley, and John Colberg took on the role of commander in the crisis. He directed all energy on the Two Dot toward holding the situation in check until law and order could be restored.

John directed Odie Foust to take in all men willing to fight the Flying C without question.

"Odie, if any man admits he's game and can sit a horse and shoot, put him on the payroll. Don't ask questions. We need everybody we can get to defeat the Flying C."

Odie nodded grimly. "I agree with you, boss. I'm taking in men on the Two Dot I normally wouldn't even consider hiring. Some of them are so old or stoved up they can barely ride. But they sure have grit and are fired up. That's enough for me."

* * *

THE WAR between the Flying C and the Two Dot had been growing steadily as the roundup season drew near. On either side of the open range, cowboys were clashing with their firearms, singly or in groups. As tensions rose, a full attack seemed inevitable. The Two Dot ranch began to take on the appearance of a military camp. Tents were pitched across the landscape and an old man with prior bugling experience was hired and provided a bugle to sound an alarm in case of an attack. There were enough men available at the main house should they need to defend against any unexpected full-out assaults by their adversaries. On the other side, the Flying C also readied themselves for a decisive battle.

The war moved into the Boulder Valley streets and saloons. Duels and shootouts took place in the town whenever opposing parties encountered one another, without warning to bystanders. No one was safe, and bullets from the warring factions injured or killed more than one innocent person. The deaths did nothing to quell the violence.

Out on the range, snipers made incursions into enemy territory and picked off lone riders. Groups of cowboys were ambushed and killed in line cabins in the mountains. The fate of many killed in the cattle war was unknown, the assailants leaving them to rot where they died, forgotten by the world. The killer or killers galloped away before they suffered the same outcome as those they vanquished. In all the chaos, the Kid reveled in it, filled with joy. The power he held and the fear he instilled in the valley's inhabitants delighted him. He was again under Calloway's protection, and he felt invincible.

Still, one thing bothered the Kid, and it bothered him a lot. His capture by John Colberg and the Two Dot cowboys was the first time the Kid had truly faced the prospect of seeing the end of a rope. And although he dismissively joked about it with Calloway and others on the Flying C, the incident spooked him. The Kid had been afraid, and that fear turned into a seething hatred for John Colberg. Odie Foust, he already despised. His thoughts sharply focused on one thing, getting the Two Dot owner in any way possible. The Kid told all who would listen that John's death was a guaranteed deal.

* * *

JOHN COLBERG'S eyes darted back and forth over the wooded foothills as he rode through them. The sun filtered through the trees, casting flickering shadows on his face. He knew that every canyon, every coulee, could be an ambush point for riders from the Flying C. He also understood that he was at the top of the Kid's list of people to eliminate. Despite the danger, he spent day after day gathering scattered cattle and patrolling the Two Dot, moving slowly and cautiously, keeping his eyes peeled for anything out of place. One wrong move or moment of inattention could mean a bullet in his back. He pressed on with his work, determined to do what he could for his ranch. Only when the last head of cattle was safely on the Two Dot would he allow himself a moment's respite.

John forbade any of his men to travel alone. They were only allowed to travel in groups large enough to discourage attacks. Still, it was impossible to keep the groups completely together as they went about their work. That provided an opportunity for a brave and enterprising opponent to attack.

John placed Odie Foust in charge of all Two Dot line camps, while he remained with the largest group of men at the main house. Odie had always proved himself invaluable to the Two Dot. He was the initial object of the Kid's wrath and he had been a brave and resourceful man when the Two Dot tried to apprehend the Kid for killing the cook. Though Odie failed, it wasn't for lack of trying. The Kid was a tough and wily character.

John frequently rode his horse between the line camps, surveying the land and talking to the men stationed there. He could feel the tension in the air, like an invisible weight that seemed to press down harder with every day that passed. The Two Dot ranch was too large for them to secure completely. They hadn't enough manpower to patrol it all, leaving plenty of opportunity for Flying C riders to sneak onto the property, drive off cattle, and get into skirmishes with Colberg's men. Injuries mounted as they battled against each other, both sides determined not to back down. John reluctantly appealed to the territorial authorities for assistance—only to find his cries fell on deaf ears. Branson Calloway held powerful influence over many people in the territory, and now he wielded that influence like a sledgehammer.

* * *

JOHN'S FACE was wrought with exhaustion as the roundup commenced, haggard from the long days and nights in the saddle. The ranch hands assembled to begin the Herculean task of trying to complete the roundup in the middle of a shooting war with the Flying C; there seemed to be little chance of success. Nonetheless, they began, led by the wearied Two Dot owner, his face a mask of determination that rallied the men around him.

As the work continued, John Colberg's horse plodded forward, as weary as his rider, his back arched in exhaustion, eyes half-closed and ears down. John hadn't been able to take a rest for days—not only was the danger relentless on the trail, but his heart weighed heavy with love for Elizabeth. He could think of little else, and he longed to reconcile with her and bring the cattle war to an end. But it felt like an impossible task—the fighting went on unabated and everything Elizabeth's father stood for and did, created a seemingly impenetrable barrier to them reconciling. The thought of a future together felt as far away as the stars John often stared at in the night sky.

John's deteriorating state affected those around him, including Odie Foust. Odie adopted a cavalier attitude about his life, often venturing into Flying C territory to cause trouble for Calloway and the Kid with little thought given to his safety.

Many cautioned him against his actions, but he just smiled at them and said, "The Kid has always had it in for me since the incident with the cook. Good people have died in this cattle war. There's no need for it. I feel duty-bound to give the Kid and Calloway as much hell as I can. Either we'll win this thing, or they'll plant me in the ground. All that matters to me is that I see this situation through to the end."

* * *

JOHN HAD COME to view Odie as a brother. They had formed an unbreakable bond through their shared experiences, confiding in each other and relying on one another for advice. As a result, John was devastated when he learned that Odie had been captured by the Kid.

The news arrived with the sound of thundering horse hooves approaching the Two Dot. From inside the ranch house, John observed a rider approaching at breakneck speed and his heart sank; something bad had happened. The rider yanked the exhausted horse to a stop in front of the house, not bothering to tether it before stumbling out of the saddle and running up to the front door.

John rushed to meet the man at the entrance to the home. He opened the door and ushered an obviously distressed Two Dot cowboy inside the dwelling. The cowboy's hands shook as he relayed the news. "The Kid captured Odie! Odie and some men were gathering cattle from the Flying C side and were on their way back to the Two Dot. It got dark, so they camped for the night. That's when the Kid struck, catching Odie and two of his men by surprise. One man got away and told us what happened. They weren't even able to fight!"

Further questioning elicited no more useful information. John dismissed the man and collapsed into a deep leather chair. He could only imagine the worst outcome for Odie. Surely the Kid had something special planned. Something painful and torturous.

THE ELKHORNS

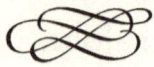

A group of men on horseback wound their way through the Elkhorn Mountains. The group was silent except for their leader's occasional whistling and singing. He sang "The Cowboy's Lament," a song he'd heard on the Flying C from cowboys who had arrived from Texas. The riders' pace was slow and steady. The terrain didn't lend itself to quick travel.

The Kid was in fine spirits. Everything was going his way, and things couldn't be better. He had gained a valuable prize, Odie Foust. He looked back at the group and smiled, noting the difficulty three men had riding their horses. The Kid had bound their feet with soft ropes, tied from ankle to ankle; the ropes passed under the horse's belly. The three men's hands were also loosely bound at the wrists. It was a dangerous situation, to be sure. If any of their horses spooked, severe injury or death was guaranteed. Despite their handicaps and difficulties, the bound men rode with confidence. It was obvious they were veteran cowmen, and they glared contemptuously at their captors as they traveled along the rough trail. Especially Odie Foust.

The riders pushed their horses up the trail, jostling and shifting in their saddles as they bounced along. After what felt like an eternity, a clearing suddenly appeared. With relief, they urged their horses forward onto the flat patch of ground. They could see up ahead that the clearing narrowed into a small box canyon. A group of massive boulders that seemed to have been carelessly tossed by an ancient giant lay strewn about the entrance. An eerie silence filled the air around Mulie Canyon, but after hours of riding, everyone was eager for a break.

The Kid and his men dismounted their horses with a thud. They untied the captives just long enough to allow them to get off their horses. Then, under the Kid's personal supervision, they were bound again by hand and foot, except Odie Foust. Odie was treated differently; being left with hands unbound, the Kid handed him a piece of paper and a crude pencil that he had taken from Branson's office.

The Kid stood in front of Odie and addressed the entire group. "I don't want anybody sayin' I killed Odie Foust without lettin' him write a letter to his mother or whoever the hell he wants to send a message to. Now, Odie, get to writing. You don't have long to live. The rest of you get those saddles off the horses and hobble them. We'll stay here a little while."

The Kid's men set about their work without comment. They knew better than to complain about his orders. It was bad for a person's health. They dropped the saddles on the ground, hobbling the horses and allowing them to graze. A campfire was built, and a man was assigned to prepare a simple meal from the meager supplies they possessed.

The Kid sat on a saddle blanket and used a saddle as a makeshift desk to compose a letter of his own. He wrote slowly and with hesitation, scratching out his writing and starting again. The Kid was proud to have enough education to pen a letter, despite his poor composition skills and spelling errors.

As for Odie, he had received an excellent education as a youth and wrote with confidence and skill. He didn't expect any mercy from the Kid. Odie was aware of the Kid's strong grudge and knew the outlaw was one to settle his scores in blood. As Odie glanced at the campfire and studied the scene, his body slumped. The men around the campfire were some of the Kid's most loyal followers. They were men who tried emulating the Kid in every action and deed. They'd been at the cabin fight, in the jail at Boulder Valley, and Odie knew they bore him a grudge almost as great as the Kid's. There'd be no possibility of help from that quarter.

Odie was shocked that they hadn't gunned him down immediately upon his capture. His mind raced as he tried to figure out the Kid's plan. Whatever the plan was, Odie was sure it involved a great deal of pain. He decided to face whatever was coming with as much dignity as possible. Odie wanted John Colberg and the Two Dot men to remember him fondly. He sighed with resignation as he realized this was probably the best he could hope for now.

Odie and the Kid both put their pencils down about the same time. The Kid slowly stood up and walked over to Odie, extending his arm with an open palm. Odie handed him his crumpled sheet of words and looked at the Kid with disdain. The Kid delicately placed both letters together and waved a man, Sleepy Jack, over from across the campfire. When Sleepy Jack staggered up, the Kid held out the letters to him and Sleepy Jack lazily took them, studying the papers from all angles, though he could barely read a word. The Kid rolled his eyes and looked at Odie with a smirk.

The Kid spoke to the Two Dot foreman loudly, so everyone could hear. "Now look here, Foust. I've decided to put off killin' you for a few hours. You're a lucky man. Don't go givin' me any trouble. Maybe you don't have to die at all. That depends on Colberg. Sleepy Jack will take your letter and mine to the Two Dot. My letter gives Colberg our location and until the morning to come and take your place. Right now, I want him more than you.

If he doesn't show up, you'll be the one headin' for the great beyond. We'll see how much he likes you."

The Kid beamed with pride at his plan. Odie lowered his head and remained silent. He knew the Kid's plan would work. The Kid had John Colberg figured out. Odie knew John wouldn't be able to resist coming to his aid and taking on the outlaw. It was his nature. All Odie could do was wait and not antagonize the Kid too much.

The camp settled into a state of lethargy as Sleepy Jack saddled his horse and prepared to leave for the Two Dot with the letters. The Kid stopped him before he left.

"Hey! Tell Colberg not to get the idea in his head to bring a bunch of men up here to fight me. You tell him that at the first sign of anybody else showing up, I'll shoot Odie down. Colberg better get here in the morning, or the Two Dot will be short a foreman. When you're done with your task, head back to the Flying C. If you need rest, coyote out somewhere safe, and head into the Flying C in the morning."

Sleepy Jack nodded and set off down the trail, his head bobbing slowly to the rhythm of his horse. The Kid started to sing "The Cowboy's Lament" quietly and walked over to the campfire. He sat down and uncorked a bottle of whiskey that was lying against a saddle, taking a long drink. The whiskey was of poor quality and the bitter liquid burned as it went down. But the Kid didn't mind; the thought of John Colberg's demise turned the bitterness to a sweet warmth. He resumed his singing and the other men, minus the captives, joined in. The soft sound of singing floated through the air and into the darkness of Mulie Canyon, the peacefulness of the sound hiding the menace that lurked behind it.

TIME

*B*ranson Calloway stepped onto the front porch of the Flying C ranch house. The sun was just cresting the mountains, and half the sky was pink while the other half was streaky swirls of purple and orange. A heavy mist coated the valley floor and made everything look as though it were under water. It was a beautiful morning. He stretched his arms and took in the panorama.

As he stretched, he heard the creak of a rocking chair to his left and glanced in that direction. Rocking in the chair slowly, was Elizabeth. She looked straight ahead and didn't acknowledge her father.

Branson smiled and said, "Good morning,

Elizabeth. What a fine day it's going to be. I see you're in your cowpuncher attire. Are you off for an early morning ride?"

Elizabeth didn't answer, and Branson looked at her closer. He noticed the tears streaming down her face and his smile disappeared.

"Hey, what's the matter? Why are you shedding tears on a day like this?"

Elizabeth continued staring straight ahead, pursed her lips, and said, "Damn you and damn this cattle war. Everything is messed up."

Branson took a step back. "Hold your tongue, girl! Is that any way to talk to your father?"

Elizabeth replied petulantly, "I'll talk to you how I please! I'm not a little girl anymore, and your scheming will get both men I love killed."

Branson stood up straight, full of anger. "Both of the men? What do you mean? Oh, I get it! You're in love with that mangy cowboy over on the Two Dot. I knew it. I knew it when he came flying through the window that night."

Elizabeth looked her father straight in the

eyes and said, "What if I am in love with him? That's no business of yours. You haven't even attempted to do the things we discussed. My feelings mean nothing to you. All you care about is your conquests and schemes. It doesn't matter who gets hurt. I don't know what my mother saw in you."

Branson was taken aback. He hadn't experienced this level of anger from his daughter before, and he didn't know how to respond. He angrily pointed his finger at her and spoke as though he were talking to a young child. "Now you listen to me, young lady!"

That's all Branson got out of his mouth before Elizabeth leaped off the rocking chair as if propelled by a spring and rushed from the porch. Her feet pounded against the dirt as she sprinted to the stables, her heart racing in time with her footsteps. Branson stood frozen in place, stunned. Elizabeth reappeared on her horse a short time later. With determination in her eyes, she spurred the steed into a wild gallop and was gone.

Elizabeth's sudden departure shook Branson out of his trance. He rushed to the bunkhouse and threw open the door. The cowboys inside stopped mid-conversation as their boss barreled into the room. Coffee mugs and plates of bacon rested on the table, and each man sat straight in their chairs, watching Branson warily. His gaze landed on Abe Finnegan, the cowboy who was usually assigned to shadow Elizabeth when she went riding in the hills. He was a quiet and unassuming man that Branson trusted him implicitly.

Branson spoke with urgency. "Abe, get your horse saddled. Elizabeth just left in a hurry. She's all riled up and left here on the run. I suspect she's headed for the Two Dot. Get moving! She'll have to slow her horse at some point. She can't run the animal all the way to the Two Dot. You should be able to catch up with her."

Finnegan leaped from the table, grabbed his gear, and was soon off to gather his horse. Branson returned to the ranch house and waited outside until he saw Finnegan head out on his task. He then returned to his office.

* * *

WHILE WAITING for Finnegan to return, Branson paced back and forth, his hands wringing in agitation as he thought of the events that had unfolded earlier. Elizabeth's tantrum had been so intense that even the cattle seemed to have felt it. And then she had declared her love for John Colberg, something Branson hadn't seen coming. He was concerned about what would happen next and how he could best protect his daughter. Branson knew one thing for certain; Elizabeth was all he had left since his wife passed and he couldn't bear to lose her.

A couple of hours went by before a knock sounded in Branson's office, and he heard the maid's voice through the wooden door. "Mr. Finnegan is here, sir," she said. Branson left his desk with a sigh, already sure that something was wrong. He followed her down the hallway and into the sitting parlor, where Abe Finnegan waited. The man stood near the fire, hands stuffed in his pockets, gaze averted toward the floorboards.

Branson addressed the cowman impatiently. "Well, Abe. What news do you have? Is Elizabeth here?"

Finnegan shook his head, still looking at

the floor. He knew his boss would not be happy with the news he was about to deliver. "No, sir. She done took off toward the Elkhorns."

Branson couldn't help himself and he yelled at Abe, "The Elkhorns! Why would she do that? You were supposed to keep track of her! You fell down on the job, mister. What happened?"

Abe looked slowly at Branson, afraid of what might happen, and answered, "I followed her just like you wanted, Mr. Calloway. I swear I did, and I caught up to her quickly. She must've slowed her horse considerably after she left."

He swallowed hard and continued, "Anyway, I laid back from her, following. I don't know if she knew I was out there or not. We went up the trail a bit when I spied a rider ahead. She saw him too and approached him.

"At first, I was a little spooked by her doing that, and I closed the distance, wanting to get to her if need be. I realized the rider was one of the Kid's men, Sleepy Jack. I knew it because of the mangy, flea-bitten gray he rides and his lazy manner in the saddle. They talked for a bit, and then Elizabeth galloped off toward the Elkhorns."

Abe rubbed his whiskers and paused, waiting for a reaction from Branson. None came; Branson glowered at him but was silent.

He continued with his story, a little more confidence in his voice. "I galloped up to Sleepy Jack to get a handle on the situation. He told me the Kid was up on that flat spot right before Mulie Canyon. The Kid has Odie Foust and a couple of men held captive up there. Said the Kid forced John Colberg's hand, and that Colberg was headed up there by himself to save his foreman. He also said the Kid meant to kill Colberg as soon as he showed up. I figured I better get back here and tell you right away. I can tell you Elizabeth has at least a rifle with her, so she's armed. She's a crack shot, you know."

Branson thought for a moment.

"Abe, gather what men you can get around here. Get them rigged and ready to go. I'll get my gear and horse ready. We're headin' for the Elkhorns. I've screwed up badly. I need to fix this situation. Now. Don't stand around! Get moving!"

It wasn't long before Branson, along with his men, tore out of the Flying C at full speed. It all boiled down to time.

* * *

ELIZABETH SLOWED her horse to a walk a short while after racing from the Flying C. The horse was winded and sweating heavily. She felt embarrassed and patted the horse lovingly on the neck. It wasn't right to take out her feelings on the animal.

I'm sorry I took out my frustration on you. You didn't do anything. I'm just so darn mad right now. Everything is jumbled up. I can't stop worrying about John or my father. That's right, Elizabeth. Admit it to yourself. You've been hiding your feelings inside and trying to deny them. You do love John Colberg. Accept it and get used to it. Well, I did just blurt it out to my father. That probably wasn't the right time for that! Dad might disown me for it, but I must be true to myself. I'm a grown woman, not a child. The problem is ... I don't know how to fix this mess. Fix it, so nobody else gets hurt.

Elizabeth rode on slowly toward the Two Dot. She didn't know what to do or say when she arrived. She even fancied they might take her prisoner and hold her until the war was resolved. It didn't make any difference; her feelings compelled her to head in that direction.

She'd been on the trail for about an hour when she spied a rider ahead. She was immediately on guard, but as she drew closer, she recognized the horse.

Oh, one of the Kid's men. It must be Sleepy Jack. He's the only one who rides a flea-bitten gray like that. The horse is steady, but it sure looks bad. At least Jack isn't the worst of the Kid's men. He's a little slow in the head, though. What's he doing here all by himself? That's unusual. If he were raiding, there'd be more people with him. I'll stop him and find out what he's up to.

Elizabeth rode up to Sleepy Jack and both riders stopped, facing each other.

Elizabeth spoke pleasantly. "Good morning, Jack. What are you doing out here all alone? Isn't that a little dangerous, given the circumstances?"

"Good morning, Miss Calloway. I could probably ask you the same question. Does your pa know where you are? A man is shadowin' you from behind. I seen him straight off. I figured it was one of your pa's men sent to monitor you."

Elizabeth was surprised at that news, but it didn't slow down her interrogation of Jack. She added a little bite to her voice. "Don't worry about me, Jack. What's your business out here? If you don't tell me, I'll be sure to tell my father you're sneaking around without his orders. Up to no good. You know I'll do it."

Sleepy Jack raised a hand in protest. "Now, don't be doin' something like that, Miss Calloway. The Kid sent me on an errand. I'm acting on his direction."

"Get it out, Jack! I don't have all day."

Sleepy Jack looked away for a moment, unhappy with his current predicament, then spoke. "The Kid's got Odie Foust prisoner up on the flat by Mulie Canyon. He gave me two letters to deliver to John Colberg at the Two Dot. I'll tell you what! I wasn't sure I was going to live! When the Two Dot boys saw me, they came at me hard. I had an old handkerchief with some white on it, so I waved it around in the air."

Jack pantomimed his surrender. Elizabeth nearly laughed at the man's exaggerated movements. She had never seen Sleepy Jack so lively.

Sleepy Jack's voice took on a more animated tone. "I guess they understood what I was gettin' at because they slowed and didn't shoot at me. I told them my business for being on the Two Dot and that Foust's life depended on me deliverin' my letters to Colberg. I also told them if any harm came to me comin' or leavin', that would also be the end of Foust. They believed me and escorted me into the ranch house, and I gave the letters to Colberg.

"Once Colberg read the Kid's letter, he set the letters on a table and told me to get the hell off his ranch before he put a bullet in me. I obliged him! The gist of the situation is that the Kid wants Colberg to take Foust's place. The Kid means to kill Colberg. You know as well as I that when he gets his mind set on something, it's likely to happen."

Sleepy Jack paused, thinking about what the Kid would have done to him had he failed in his mission.

"I cleared the Two Dot late, after dark, and was so tired I camped out. I laid up in some trees and set out for the Flying C this morning. That's the truth of it, Miss Calloway."

Elizabeth stiffened in the saddle and looked toward the Elkhorns.

She was worried and her voice took on a higher pitch than normal. "Damn the Kid! That dirty dog! I must get up there and help John. I think I can get there in time. We're a lot closer to the Elkhorns than he is."

Without another word, Elizabeth spurred her horse and took off toward the Elkhorns.

* * *

JOHN COLBERG RECEIVED the letters from Sleepy Jack late in the afternoon. He only read the Kid's letter. Odie's private letter to his kin, he left alone. That was none of his business. Besides, Odie would live if he had any say in the matter.

The ride to Mulie Canyon was much further from the Two Dot than the Flying C. John knew he had to get on the trail in due haste to make it in time. He decided he'd lay up on the trail once it got dark and set out again at first light. The last part of the trail was too dangerous to pass at night. Still, John knew the Kid meant every word he'd written. Time was of the essence.

John left the ranch house without telling anyone the Kid had captured Odie. He couldn't risk anyone following him. He told a trusted cowboy that he had to run an errand in Boulder Valley and would be back in the morning. John clarified he was going alone and wouldn't need any assistance. He saddled his horse, packed a few provisions, and slipped away from the Two Dot.

He followed the winding trail until it stopped at the base of the climb to Mulie Canyon. It would be dark soon and it was time to stop for the night. John unsaddled his horse and let it graze in the patchy grass nearby. While gathering kindling to build a fire, he remembered the bottle of whiskey he had packed. Although he rarely indulged, the drink seemed like a good way to calm his mind a bit.

John dropped the kindling and retrieved the whiskey bottle from a saddlebag. He pulled the cork, then took two quick drinks from the bottle, feeling the liquid's warmth coat his insides as it trickled down his throat. The sensation was reassuring; it didn't bring happiness, but it brought relief. He abandoned the idea of building a campfire and chose to sit against a tree, sipping from the bottle, thinking.

I'm tired. So tired. Calloway and the Kid are relentless. Maybe I won't make it out of this deal. What's the Kid's game? Is this a trap, and he means to kill us both when I show up? He isn't exactly honest, that's for sure. It doesn't matter. I must do something, even if it leads to my death. I want people to say I at least tried to change things. At least I tried to save my friend. I wonder what Elizabeth is doing right now? I wish I could see her one more time. I guess that's not in the cards. I better try to get some rest; tomorrow is likely to be one helluva day.

Feeling the whiskey and the weight of his fatigue, John laid out his bedroll. He propped his head against his saddle and settled in for the night. Sleep came, but it was fitful and sporadic.

RESOLUTION

*J*ohn set out for Mulie Canyon as the faint blush of dawn tinged the sky. He picked his way carefully along the rocky, winding trail as the morning dew glistened off the needles on the pine trees. His horse breathed hard against the steepening climb, occasionally snorting with the effort. John slackened the reins and gave the horse the bit, letting the animal do its work. The brightening sun began to warm his back, the heat slowly spreading throughout his body. He began to hum a tune in time to the horse's gait, unaware that further down the mountain a young woman had started her trek up the trail, closing the distance between them.

The rhythm of the ride made John sleepy, and he had almost dozed off when he heard someone call from the woods. Two men on horses appeared from the trees on either side of the trail.

One man shouted out, "Hey, Colberg! Keep your pistol holstered and don't try anything. The Kid sent us to escort you the rest of the way to camp. Pass by us, and we'll ride behind you."

John raised a hand to let the men know he understood their directions. He continued up the trail and passed them without looking at either one. They filed in behind, and the group plodded on its way in silence.

* * *

THE MORNING WAS chilly in the camp; the warmth of the morning sun came late to the mountains' recesses, and frost had formed overnight on the grass. Odie Foust, bound again shortly after writing his letter, and his two men remained in that condition through the night, partially covered with thin blankets. They were stiff, numb, and shivering as the morning grew later.

The Stipic Kid had slept well next to a fire his men tended periodically overnight. He was in a festive mood and whistled and sang as breakfast was prepared. He occasionally glanced over at Odie and laughed.

Odie had slept with his back against a large tree, and he straightened a little and gazed at the peaks shining in the morning sun. Sunlight was spreading over the small clearing, but it hadn't reached him yet. The Kid's obvious glee at his discomfort didn't bother him, and he focused on nature's beauty. It was likely the last thing he'd see in his life. He worried about the state of the two men next to him. They were sullen and seemed to have lost hope.

He'd been looking at the mountain peaks for a few moments when he realized there was no more singing at the campfire. Odie looked in that direction and saw the Kid staring at him.

The Kid taunted Odie, "Take in that pretty view, Foust. Look at it hard. It's likely the last thing you'll ever see in this world. The mornin' is passing by, and Colberg is nowhere to be seen. That doesn't bode well for you."

Odie chuckled and replied defiantly, "I sure as hell hope he doesn't show up. As for you, you might think you're smart, but I don't think you are. You're just a half-wit killer, and people like you always meet their end the same way: at the end of a rope or lyin' out in the hills as food for the coyotes. You don't scare me, Kid. You might kill me, but you don't scare me."

Usually, the Kid would laugh at such talk, but Odie's open contempt cut him deep. The Kid jumped to his feet and stared at the Two Dot foreman. A tic worked in his left eye and his hand went to the pistol at his side, his knuckles whitening as he squeezed the weapon hard. All activity around the campfire ceased, and the only sound was the crackling of the fire as all eyes turned to the Kid. The outlaw stood frozen for what seemed like an eternity to those watching him. Then, the Kid released a breath he had been holding and relaxed, breaking into an exaggerated laugh. He slowly released his hand from his weapon.

The Kid shook a finger at Odie. "I know

what you're up to, Foust. You're trying to bait me into shootin' you, thinking I'll spare Colberg. It ain't gonna work. You won't trick me that easily. Hell, I'm willing to wait here all day just so you can watch me put some bullets in your boss. Then it might be your turn if you don't quit runnin' that mouth."

The Kid then turned to the man cooking breakfast.

"Get me some breakfast. I'm feelin' mighty hungry. Foust and his buddies don't get anything. You hear?"

The man prepared a plate for the Kid, and soon everyone around the campfire was gobbling the meager meal. Odie and his men watched the outlaws eating and hung their heads. The sense of despair deepened among Odie's group.

Not long after they finished breakfast, a call came from the edge of the clearing where it joined the trail down the mountain. Soon after, John Colberg appeared, followed by his two escorts. The Kid remained seated at the fire, watching the riders approach the camp.

When the riders reached the campfire, the Kid rose to his feet and did a little jig.

He moved close to Colberg and said, "I'll

be. You do have some sand, Colberg. I was startin' to worry you wouldn't show. You may have saved Odie's life, although it's difficult to say. These situations are always up in the air."

John glared at the Kid. "Let Odie and the men go. That was the deal."

The Kid grinned, thoroughly enjoying the situation. "What's the hurry? Get off that horse and relax a little around the fire. We don't have any food left, but there's a little coffee. Have a sip."

The Kid pulled out his pistol and leveled it at the Two Dot boss. John reluctantly dismounted from his horse and joined the Kid at the campfire. He looked over at Odie and grimaced. John's worry was clear, and it made the Kid smirk.

One of the Kid's men handed John a tin cup filled with coffee. He stared at the dark liquid, swirling it in the cup, but didn't drink any. The cup's warmth soothed his stiff hands but did little to ease his troubled thoughts. John's mind was occupied with calculating if there was any possibility of escaping the situation. Frankly, he didn't see any way out of the predicament except for death. Still, the longer the Kid lingered, the better. Maybe things would turn in his favor. He had to stay calm and think.

* * *

ELIZABETH PUSHED her horse up the trail hard. Too hard. The horse was exhausted and giving out. Still, she urged the animal onward. There was no time to lose, not if she wanted to save John.

She knew she must be close to the flat by Mulie Canyon. Elizabeth heard the talking and laughter of men clearly in the mountain air. She couldn't make out anything they said, but occasionally, the Kid's high voice was recognizable. It was impossible to tell from the voices exactly where the men were in the clearing. Sometimes the voices seemed close, sometimes far away.

Elizabeth gently pulled on the reins and felt her horse slow and gradually come to a stop beneath her. She put her weight onto a stirrup, swung her leg over the saddle and slid off, landing softly on the ground. She grabbed the reins and tugged to get the horse moving again, keeping an eye on the trail for a secluded spot that would do for tying it up.

At last, she found one and guided the horse off the path and into the sheltering arms of the forest. Elizabeth pulled her Henry rifle from the scabbard, loading a cartridge in the chamber swiftly before resting the hammer back down. All was still as she surveyed her surroundings.

The forest was thick, and the last bit of the hill up to the clearing was steep. It wouldn't be easy to move quietly in the dense forest, but it had to be done. She hastily formulated a plan in her mind.

It's going to be tough to reach the clearing's edge without making too much noise. I'm hoping I have the element of surprise on my side, and they aren't expecting anyone other than John to show up. Is he up there right now? It sure seems like they're having a good time.

This Henry gives me a fair range for shooting. I should be able to get close enough to cover the area I need. I'll go to the right and sneak up the hill to the edge. Find a nice resting place for the rifle and wait for a good shot at the Kid. He's the key. The rest of the bunch might take off if I can get the Kid. At least, that's what I hope will happen.

Elizabeth moved stealthily through the

trees, like a cat closing in on its prey. She made a little noise, but it alerted no one in the camp. Once she reached the edge of the clearing, she made out John sitting at the campfire with the Kid. Behind them, against some trees, she could see Odie and two other men.

She saw that Odie and his men were bound, but they didn't seem to be in a great deal of distress or immediate danger. John was unbound and relaxed at the campfire. She judged the distance to the men to be well within shooting range, and she delicately moved behind a large fallen tree. She rested the rifle on the tree, pulled the hammer back and aimed at the Kid. The somewhat casual appearance of the scene confused her. What was going on? She relaxed her aim and lowered the hammer. Elizabeth decided to wait a little, see how things played out.

* * *

THE KID CONTINUED to sing and joke with his men. He'd occasionally direct remarks to John, but the Two Dot owner said nothing in return, deliberately ignoring his nemesis.

Then, without warning, the Kid's mood changed.

"Alright, boys. Enough of this foolin' around. The day's getting late, and we need to take care of our business. Get over there and untie Foust and his men."

The Kid's men moved fast, quickly untangling the ropes that bound the captives. The Kid and John followed closely behind, with the Kid holding his gun at arm's length, its aim fixed directly on John. Odie and his two companions groaned as they rose from the ground, their muscles aching from being tied for so long.

Odie looked at the Kid. "Let John go. Take me instead."

The Kid shook his head. "Sorry, Foust. I can't do that. I promised Colberg to shoot him instead of you if he showed up. I'm a man who keeps his word. Of course, I can always shoot you, too, if that's what you want."

John walked over to Odie, and gave him a pat on the back, trying to comfort his foreman.

"It's OK, Odie. Don't worry. I need a good man to look after the Two Dot. Promise me you'll look after the place and keep it going right once I'm gone."

Odie looked at his boss, and softly said, "I sure will, John. I promise I'll catch up with you when I cross over to the other side."

John shook hands with the other Two Dot men, then moved to the big pine tree where Odie and the two cowboys had sat throughout the night. The Kid watched, indifferent, and was about to tell John to turn and face him when the shouts of several men came from the edge of the clearing.

Back in the trees, Elizabeth was about to pull the trigger when she also heard the shouts. She paused, wondering who would appear. Was it her father? It had to be him. The man shadowing her must have returned to the Flying C to report her activities.

The Kid and his men turned toward the shouts, on guard. Several men from the Flying C tore into the clearing, led by a tall, gaunt man in a long black frock coat.

Branson Calloway thundered up to the Kid on his horse, its hooves sending a cloud of dust skyward. He pulled hard on the reins, bringing the animal to a sliding stop. Branson leaped to the ground and stood defiantly in front of the Kid, hands on his hips. His men drew their guns and circled round like hawks, hungry and ready to devour any trouble that came their way.

Branson spoke firmly. "It's over, Kid. The cattle war is over. The shooting is done. I've been a darn fool and seen the error of my ways. Stand down and tell your men to do the same."

The Kid knew it was over. He didn't dare challenge Calloway. Branson had too much power, and the Kid knew any challenge to that power would end badly for him. The only thing left was survival, and that meant leaving Boulder Valley. He didn't relish calling it quits, but staying alive was always his top priority. There would be plenty of other places where he could work his outlaw trade. No need to risk dying here. It wasn't worth it. His cold mind worked on a solution to his new problem.

The Kid looked around at his men and said, "You heard the boss, boys. Stand down. We ride for the Flying C brand."

The Kid's men looked at one another, surprised. They had a hard time believing the Kid would give up without a fight, but none of them was going to challenge his order. They all holstered their guns and stood silently, wondering what would happen next.

Branson studied the Kid warily for a moment, then approached John and held out his hand. John took it cautiously, and the two men shook hands.

"It's over, Colberg. Let's call a truce in this war. I'm not losing my daughter over a fight for land and cattle. She means too much to me. I realize that now. An empire isn't worth a cent if you lose the people you love in building it. We can work out the details of making things right later. By the way, where's Elizabeth? She took off in this direction early this morning."

John looked puzzled. "I haven't seen her. She didn't show up here, thankfully."

Just as soon as John finished speaking, Elizabeth stepped out of the trees. She ran toward the group of men at full speed, the soles of her boots barely skimming the grass of the clearing. Without a word, she ran up to John, and dropped her rifle on the ground beside him. She lunged at him and threw her arms around him in a tight embrace, kissing him. John was so surprised he didn't reciprocate immediately. He stood there woodenly for a few seconds, doing nothing. Then he relaxed and embraced Elizabeth tightly.

Branson rolled his eyes and shook his head in disbelief. "Who would've thought such a thing could happen? I sure as hell didn't."

John's mood suddenly changed, and his eyes flashed with rage as he abruptly released Elizabeth and started toward the Kid with long, determined strides. He clenched his fists and his jaw, his eyes fixed on the Kid; he intended to do the outlaw harm. Branson reacted without a second thought, throwing himself between John and the Kid.

He spread out open palms in protest and shouted, "Hold on there, Mr. Colberg! The Kid is my business and mine alone. It looks like you have a pretty full plate on your hands. You best tend to that business and leave me to mine."

John stared coldly at the Kid, then reluctantly turned away and returned to Elizabeth.

Branson addressed the Kid. "I'll give you a day's ride head start. I figure that oughta cover the rest of the wages I owe you and your men. After that, I'll ensure men are on your trail."

The Kid nodded in agreement to the terms and said, "I reckon that'll do just fine. Come on, boys. Let's get on the move."

The Kid turned to John and pointed. "You better sleep with one eye open, Colberg. You never know when I might return to this country."

The Kid and his men gathered their belongings and set off on their horses.

Elizabeth approached her father and angrily said, "How could you just let the Kid ride off like that?"

Branson remained calm and explained, "Elizabeth, a man in my situation can't hand over hired men like the Kid to the law. There'd be consequences. Don't worry. The Kid is as good as dead now. I'll make sure he is hunted hard from now on. He doesn't stand a chance."

THE KID'S END

John and Elizabeth strolled around the Two Dot ranch hand in hand. Elizabeth's year-long absence had brought changes to the place, just as it had changed her. Flowers adorned the front of the house now, while a garden thrived out back. Elizabeth surveyed the home's new domesticity and couldn't help but laugh.

"My goodness, John. I never took you for the gardening type. Flowers and all. It looks downright homey."

John blushed, a little embarrassed. He quickly recovered and defended himself. "Well, I thought it would be a nice touch for a sophisticated lady like yourself. I had plenty of time to work on it while you were away getting your education. Besides, this will be your home soon. It needs to look right. Though I like you better in cowboy gear than a fancy dress."

Elizabeth smiled; this was the kind of banter she enjoyed between them. "Don't worry about that, cowpuncher. I haven't forgotten how to sit on a horse or rope and shoot. I just added another dimension to myself. It'll keep you on your toes."

John had tried to hide his enthusiasm for gardening from the rest of the cowboys on the Two Dot, pretending it was an obligatory task he had to do for his fiancée. But the truth was that he was proud of the work he did, and that pride showed as he pointed out his handiwork to Elizabeth.

"I selected each of these flowers carefully, and they'll make a bouquet for our wedding. It's only a month away, you know."

Elizabeth feigned offense. "I know. A lady of my educational standing would never forget such a thing. Do you remember the first time I rode in here? For Jim Webster's funeral? There wasn't a flower in sight. I must've looked like a pretty strange figure arriving here."

John nodded vigorously in mock agreement, saying, "You're a bit strange, that's for sure."

Elizabeth punched him in the arm.

John grabbed his arm as though he were in great pain. "Hey! That's not very ladylike. I doubt they taught you that in your fancy finishing school."

Elizabeth laughed and said firmly, "Mind your manners, Mr. Colberg."

She then paused, taking in the whole valley around them. "The valley sure looks peaceful and prosperous now. I've never seen it look this good. It feels different too. You can feel it in the air itself."

John knew the quiet, prosperous nature the valley had taken on since the end of the cattle war would surprise Elizabeth. Bygones were bygones. Branson made restitution to those he had harmed and, at least by outward appearances, seemed to conduct himself within the confines of the law. Some wanted Branson's head, but he was too powerful. Life is often unfair, and those that wanted him gone had to grit their teeth and accept the situation.

The Flying C became an open station for those passing through the valley, and any travelers who needed respite were welcome to rest there. For the first time since Branson Calloway had arrived in the valley, people could come and go without fear of harm. The Flying C and the Two Dot coexisted peacefully, and all the valley's inhabitants eagerly looked to the future.

* * *

THE RESIDENTS of Boulder Valley would not get the revenge against the Kid they so desperately wanted. But life has a way of sorting things out, and the Stipic Kid would meet his end in an unexpected way.

The Kid and his men were hunted relentlessly once they left the territory. Nevertheless, they left a trail of death and misery wherever they went. One by one, they had been picked off by bullets and disease until only the Kid was left.

The Kid's last-ditch plan was to ride to Old Mexico and lie low for a while. He headed south, even though he didn't know the country. He took what he needed by force and shot those who stood in his way. There were a couple of close calls before he got into a scrape in Raton, New Mexico Territory, and suffered a leg wound that became infected. Along with a rotten tooth, the injury forced the Kid to stop for rest more frequently. His last stop found him resting in a washed-out area beneath a small ledge in a sandstone cliff.

* * *

DARKNESS HAD JUST LIFTED from the desert when a posse approached the sleeping figure. The sleeping man's horse was hobbled and peacefully scrounged whatever sustenance it could take from the harsh landscape. The animal raised its head at the group's approach but made no sound and went back to eating like nothing was out of order. The men inched closer, and their leader silently signaled for them to form a semicircle around the man.

The posse leader lifted his arm and the men around him obediently readied their weapons. He stepped closer, raised his gun with a steady hand, and the synchronized clack of hammers being drawn back echoed in the air. The figure beneath the blanket stirred and opened his eyes, rubbing them for a moment before looking at the group. Unmoved by this show of force, he casually slipped one hand under his threadbare coverlet.

The posse leader spoke first. "I'm guessing you're the man called the Stipic Kid."

The Kid stared at the man coldly, but appeared relaxed and nonchalantly said, "You woke me from a good sleep. That's kinda rude. Don't you think? I haven't had a good sleep for days. Where am I? Texas?"

The posse leader was puzzled by the Kid's casual attitude. He had not seen a man take a situation like this so lightly. "No. You're in the New Mexico Territory. We're here for a murder you committed in Raton. We've been on your trail for a while now."

The Kid seemed surprised by this news. "Raton? I don't know this country well, boys. I was trying to get to Old Mexico, but it looks like I'm in New Mexico. I thought I was at least in Texas."

"Nope, Kid. You came up a little short. You killed the husband of Mrs. Walters up north of here in Raton. They run the apothecary there, or at least they did. There's only her and the children now."

The Kid's face lit up. "Oh! I remember now. All I wanted was some medicine for this bad tooth of mine. It's been hurtin' me something fierce. I was a little short on money, and the fool husband wouldn't give me the medicine. It was a bad decision on his part. All he had to do was hand it over to me. How would that've hurt him? The medicine didn't work, anyway."

The posse leader was stunned at the Kid's lack of remorse. In fact, it angered him, but he stayed calm. "We talked to Mrs. Walters, and she claimed she got a shot off at you and hit you. We didn't believe her because she's still alive."

The Kid chuckled and shook his head, finding amusement in his predicament. "I don't shoot women or children. Can you believe that? But she sure as hell shot at me. Hit me in the leg. Must have taken a bit off the bone. The leg doesn't seem broke, but it sure has caused me some trouble. Life is funny. I've faced some tough men, and now I've been laid low by a druggist."

The posse leader's voice took on a dark tone. "You shouldn't have shot the husband. It was senseless. Now you're going to pay for it."

The Kid changed the subject. "You boys sure are good at tracking. I didn't think anyone was on my trail. I've had to slow on account of this tooth and my leg, so that's held me back a bit. I've been feverish and light-headed. It's hard to travel feeling that way. Don't know if it's the leg or tooth causing it. I'm guessing it's the leg more than anything. It doesn't really matter, though."

"You aren't that hard to follow, Kid. Will you come peacefully? It doesn't look like you have much of a choice."

The Kid grinned. "If I was in Texas, I might let you take me. Being hung in New Mexico doesn't sit well with me. You're wrong, lawman; we always have a choice in this world."

The Kid's hand shot out from under the blanket so fast it was like lightning, a gun already in his grasp. He fired off one shot, the sound piercing through the early morning air, before several other gunshots followed. In an instant, the dust settled and all that could be heard was the wind carrying the echoes of the Kid's final gunfight across the desert.

ACKNOWLEDGMENTS

Thanks to everyone who contributed to the production of this book. Especially beta reader Kim Walters, editor Emma Moylan, and the Book Cover Zone.

ABOUT THE AUTHOR

Born in El Paso, TX and raised in Eastern Montana, Everett Riggs is a lifelong fan of the Western genre and history of the Old West. He is a graduate of Montana State University, the University of Iowa, and a veteran of the Gulf War. When he is not reading and writing, he enjoys the great outdoors with his family. This is his second book.

www.ingramcontent.com/pod-product-compliance
Lightning Source LLC
Chambersburg PA
CBHW021150130626
46554CB00005B/1743

*9 7 9 8 2 1 8 2 3 8 5 0 6 *